ATL~

On

Tides of

C000157756

ATLANTIS ON THE TIDES OF DESTINY

First edition. July 17, 2019.

Copyright © 2019 Jennifer McKeithen.

ISBN: 978-1393609780

Written by Jennifer McKeithen.

Also by Jennifer McKeithen

The Antediluvian Chronicles
Atlantis On the Shores of Forever
Atlantis On the Tides of Destiny

Standalone
Shahin: Escape from Persia

Watch for more at www.jennifermckeithen.com.

Dedicated to Japheth, the love of my life, and my knight in shining armor.

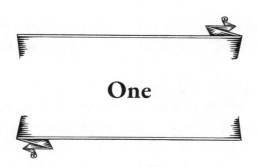

One

A CHILLED, DAMP BREEZE blew through the Broceliande forest, permeating deep into her bones. Light snow ensured the concealment of her tracks. Then the wind stopped, and all stood silent and still.

Gwenwhyfar sniffed the frozen air. Amid the acidic pine, she detected another scent. *He* was close. She could feel it. Behind crept her younger brother, Cahan. She didn't look back at him. No, she had already learned that lesson.

This winter marked her first season as a huntress. Before, she never bothered to acquire the skill, comfortable in the belief that she could leave the task to others. But the Pyrrhic victory over the Harappan invaders the previous autumn had spent her land's resources—in particular, their able-bodied men. The residents of Ker-Ys found themselves on the brink of starvation. Gwenwhyfar refused to sit by idly and permit it.

A chill shivered down her spine—and this time, it wasn't the result of the cold.

Guilt gnawed at her as she remembered the awful scene of carnage just beyond the edge of the forest boundaries. Finn, her truest friend, a man who practically worshiped her, had died there on account of her foolishness. If she hadn't insisted on taking part in the battle for Ker-Ys, he might still be alive. The horrors of war refused to leave her memory, and she began to wonder if they ever would.

She held her muscles rigid. Such dismal thoughts didn't belong in the hunt. Her people depended on their success for their next

1

meal—*she* depended on this hunt to fill her own starving belly. They had tracked the great hart from early that morning and through the rest of the day.

The sun sank low beneath the tree line. Somehow, she knew they would have their final encounter with him before night fell upon the forest. She scanned the trees around them, slowly taking in each and every detail.

From behind one of the massive oaks, she spotted him.

He held completely still, as though he hoped his pursuers wouldn't notice him among the gnarled roots and low-lying branches. Indeed, his mighty antlers were nearly indistinguishable from the tree branches in the waning light.

Out of the corner of her eye, Cahan signaled. She shook her head. They'd played that game many times.

Her younger brother relished using her to distract their prey. He would then swoop in for the felling stroke himself. No, this time she would claim the glory of the kill. All winter she had observed and learned. Spring drew nigh, and it was high time for her to have a turn.

Inching forward, she crushed the virgin snow beneath her boots. She didn't doubt Cahan fumed at her defiance. But he, too, felt the pangs of hunger, and wouldn't dare risk scaring off their next meal.

The hart peeked from behind a tree, then pulled back. He knew they followed him. But he possessed the experience of enough summers to perceive that should he bolt right away, he would surely die.

Nearing the tree, she caught his second stolen glance. Their eyes met, and for a moment she froze, transfixed by his splendor.

His eyes were the most handsome shade of brown she had ever beheld. In them, she understood that he also held the responsibility of a sovereign. Just as she ruled over Ker-Ys, he reigned as a prince of the forest Broceliande. Somewhere, deep in a hidden part of the thicket, a doe would soon give birth to his offspring, continuing his ancient and royal line.

Only one other pair of brown eyes had captivated her so.

Memories of her own people's children flooded her mind. If she let him go, some of them wouldn't stand a chance of surviving the remaining weeks until spring. The great hart must die, that her people might live.

He seemed to sense her intentions. Seizing his last chance, he fled.

Gwenwhyfar loosed her arrow.

The weapon found its mark, for its wielder had fired true. Defeated, he lay bleeding in the snow, writhing in agony. His heart was pierced, and he could run no longer.

She approached, and stooped down to one knee. "I'm sorry," she whispered in his ear, fighting back tears.

Even in the jaws of death, he was magnificent, and the forest would not know another like him during her lifetime. Unable to meet his bewitching eyes a second time, she drew her long knife across his throat, ending his suffering.

"What a shot!" Cahan exclaimed from the brush. "Perfect aim, sister. But the next one belongs to me."

A part of her wished she had missed. The eyes of that mighty beast would haunt her for months to come. But she had learned long before that she didn't have the luxury of following the desires of her heart.

Our people will eat tonight, she reminded herself.

Cahan carried the hart back to Ker-Ys on his sturdy shoulders, while she followed with the few smaller animals they'd managed to take.

Now that she found herself free from a task requiring so much concentration, her thoughts turned to Marcus Duilius, that Roman charmer who seemed to have stepped out of some heroic epic. She yearned to see him again. The memory of their first and last kiss filled her with warmth, banishing the frigid air around her.

She hadn't seen him since he'd left to report to Rome the previous autumn. The scarlet hue of his paludamentum blowing in the wind as he disappeared over the horizon lingered in her mind's eye. Not for the first time, she wondered if she'd ever see him again. This war would kill many people before it finally ended. No one could count himself as safe.

Yet she knew that even if fortune intended them both to survive this world struggle, a marriage between them would prove a far more difficult feat. Both carried the hopes and expectations of their respective families and peoples. Both had personal hopes and dreams that ran contrary to those duties and responsibilities.

The Harappans did not return after the siege, when Gwenwhyfar had fallen injured during the battle. But not before she felled the fierce warrior Finn had dubbed "Smiley." Her anger at Finn's death helped her to find a new inner strength. For the rest of her life, she vowed never to forget that she possessed such abilities, so that her bodyguard's sacrifice wouldn't be in vain.

But she needed to learn how to bring out those abilities at will, *without* drowning in the torrent of emotions that clouded her judgment.

After their victory, the remaining enemy soldiers fled into the forest, and were never seen again. She remembered their vigilance during the first few months, how her people feared to venture out to hunt on the possibility the enemy still lingered there, waiting for the right opportunity to attack a second time.

The attack never came, however, and the fate of those soldiers remained a mystery. When it came down to it, little news at all reached them from the outside world. Gwenwhyfar and her people waited, completely in the dark as to how the war went. For all they knew, they stood as the last remaining bastion of freedom in the world.

She relaxed her shoulders. *That's doubtful.* If the rest of the world had fallen, they would know about it by now, peculiar winter weather notwithstanding.

Before she knew it, they reached the gates of the city. Cahan proudly displayed their kill to the children who ran up to greet them, as though he had taken the buck down singled-handed.

The cook came out to see the hullabaloo, holding up her skirts as she waded through the snow drifts. "Brrr! It's colder out here than I realized—Oh! Look at the size of that hart! Haven't seen one that big since I was a girl. Cahan, my boy, you truly are your father's son." She pinched his cheek.

Cahan grinned, basking in the praise. "Gwenwhyfar helped."

No one heard his confession, and he didn't repeat it. Gwenwhyfar shook her head and chuckled. She would let her little brother have his fun today. But the next time, he would have to give credit where it was due.

"Maybe next time you'll catch that whale of a boar," the cook continued. "That one has roamed the forest since I was a girl, and no one can catch him..." She babbled on giddily about the feast they would all enjoy the next day, and how she would prepare the meat they brought.

Gwenwhyfar didn't stay to listen. She would not speak it aloud, but she couldn't bear to see her magnificent hart gutted, skinned, and chopped to pieces. People filled the great hall. Many had lost their homes as a result of fire and other war damage. Rebuilding was quite impossible until spring. Repeated snows obstructed any progress, and when they melted, the resulting water damage proved greater than the destruction by flames. Until then, the common rooms of the castle had been opened to those refugees for the winter.

Upon reaching her chamber, she fell into bed and pulled the furs over her head to ward off the cold.

She had much to think about. Preparations had to be made for her upcoming voyage to Atlantis. Furthermore, there remained the task of finding additional manpower in order to defend their lands against future attacks. Despite the cold, spring drew nigh, and with the new awakening would come a fresh wave of warfare. Ker-Ys must be ready. Tierney needed her to help him think of solutions.

Ever in the back of her mind lay the quandary of the dashing Marcus Duilius, distracting her from her obligations.

She would find solutions to all of those problems. But first, she needed to sleep.

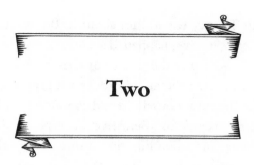

Two

GWENWHYFAR SIPPED A warm cup of her brother's mead while watching the snow fall outside. From her window, she could see the partially frozen tide pool gardens in the courtyard below.

While food stores in Ker-Ys ran short of late, a generous supply of mead remained enough to see them through until summer. Beekeepers and holy men claimed that those who drank mead were as strong as those who ate large quantities of meat. No one could say for sure why this was so, but bees did have a certain magical quality about them. Indeed, many believed the method of brewing of mead came from the gods. That the citizens of Ker-Ys had borne out the harsh winter with few casualties seemed to prove the belief.

Cahan enjoyed beekeeping and making mead from the royal hives. After hunting, it was his favorite occupation. He spent a year on the island of the Druids as a youth, where he learned the sacred arts of keeping bees and mead making. From the Druids, he acquired the secret of rendering the bees docile, so that they wouldn't sting him when he collected their honey. His assistants, on the other hand, always needed to wear the protective netting.

Gwenwhyfar grinned into her cup.

No one would let Cahan forget the first time he made a batch of mead on his own. Still perfecting the secret techniques imparted to him, he ended up getting stung all over his body when he dug up the hive to throw into his brewing pot. He lied ill in bed for a week afterward. Even Tierney teased him about it. But whatever he'd done wrong or forgotten, it never happened again.

Tradition dictated that the royalty of Ker-Ys send a member from each generation to learn the art in order to supervise the brewing of the beverage for the royal household and common people. The Druids made a different recipe for themselves, a type of drink used for inspiration quests and divining the future. Only those of their brotherhood knew that recipe. Like the Norsemen, the Breizhians made their mead from the entire hive: honey, wax, and the bees themselves.

She frowned. She *must* help her brothers think of solutions to their quandary.

Spring approached, and with it followed the threat of another invasion. They hadn't completed the repairs on the fortress walls, or recruited and trained the necessary number of warriors to defend the walls. In a way, it exhibited a favor of fortune that the Harappans kept the rest of the world busy fortifying or outright defending themselves. Otherwise, Ker-Ys in her weakened state would prove an easy a target for her neighboring rivals.

Taking another sip of her mead, she imagined her city as a beehive awakening after a long winter's slumber. Her people inherited the art of beekeeping as one of Atlantis' exiled tribes. Though now practiced for the most part in rural areas of the island continent, the Atlanteans kept a system of beehives in the Hanging Gardens for pollination purposes.

Her mind traveled to the great library, and the secret passageway she and Ptah discovered there. Had the captain gone back to find the answers he sought? What explanations did Mayor Werta offer him?

"Atlantis," she whispered.

She swirled the liquid around in her cup, unable to think of another solution now that this idea had taken hold. For food, she must go to Atlantis. No other ally demonstrated a willingness or ability to spare their resources with a tiny and insignificant kingdom. Ker-Ys possessed little to offer in return for such help.

The prospect of asking for help humiliated her as much as anyone else. But for the sake of her people, she would swallow her pride. Werta wouldn't lord it over her, at least. Her people couldn't live on mead forever—or at least, she didn't care to test the theory. Not even the Druids did it, despite their claim it was possible.

The Druids.

Why hadn't she thought to consult the Druids? True, they only allowed visitors to their island on certain ritual days, or in times of special need. This was most definitely a time of great need. The sixth day following the full moon had already passed, so there was no danger of her interrupting their ritual harvesting of the sacred mistletoe.

She took another sip, pondering how the forces of the Otherworlds influenced her natural world, how even the Harappans must serve as mere puppets to these forces. Fortunate indeed Ker-Ys must be, to posses the favor of the mother goddess' protection. Without her goodwill, the less benevolent denizens of those realms might have overrun and destroyed her city long ago.

The Druids would demand something in return for their counsel. Little food remained, but she decided the benefits of their wisdom outweighed the cost. Besides, she intended to depart for Atlantis immediately afterward and return soon with more food.

She summoned a messenger.

MIST HUNG IN BELTS around the tiny island just off the shores of Ker-Ys. Woods of oak and holly covered the island. Small rabbits and birds roamed about the gentle slopes and hills of its interior without fear of predators. Hardly enough game to feed the number of people who dwelt there.

The island's only human inhabitants were the Druids, priests of the ancient gods. They lived as hermits, growing their facial hair into long, wispy beards, and wearing robes of rough, woven wool. Even the savage Venetii heeded the council of these wise sages.

With trepidation, Gwenwhyfar paddled her tiny boat through the calm, yet freezing waters. She did not remember visiting this island before, though Tierney said their mother brought her there as an infant for a blessing. She floated nearer to the shore, and those tall, dark trees and mysterious shadows mirrored the sense of foreboding hanging over her, pressing like a weight on her chest.

A flock of seabirds on the beach squalled away at her approach. Everyone knew of her arrival now. She imagined the priests would greet her with something like, "We knew you were coming."

Swallowing hard, she stepped out of her boat. Cold salt water seeped into her boots. To the south, she saw the smoke of their campfires rising above the treeline, where the inhabitants made their homes. She made her way toward the trees.

Past the trees was a clearing, where the Druids hovered in their places around an enchanted millpond, awaiting her. Like most, she believed these priests possessed the gift of direct guidance from faefolk and beings who dwelt in the Otherworlds. Cahan told her the Druids spent hours at the pond's edge, listening through the water across time and space.

Only in times of great need did the ethereal servants of the gods make use of the watery gateways to cross over into the natural realm. Of course, the gods themselves determined the degree of any necessary, of when and where they decided to intervene in mortal affairs.

"Gwenwhyfar, daughter of the Breizhians," greeted the leader. "We've been expecting you."

She wondered if they simply said that to everyone who came to their island, or if they truly did see the future before it came to pass.

But she didn't dare voice that question. The gods would not give her answers if she expressed a lack of faith in their representatives.

"Make your offering, child," he instructed, "then state your business." His tone was kind, though his expression blank.

She threw a handful of incense into the fire. For the Druids themselves, she lowered her sack from her shoulder, which contained a leg of the stag she had killed.

"I seek your advice," she began. "I don't know how to defend my people from our enemies and their evil deities. So many of our men have been killed in the recent siege that I must find new allies. But I don't know where or how to find them."

He considered her words for a moment, then turned to communicate silently with his brothers. When they reached an agreement, he turned back to her. "We cannot give you direct advice in matters of war. We can only give you a direction in which to proceed."

She bowed her head. "I will listen." They chanted a few prayers together, then the youngest left their circle to speak to her. She surmised he was an acolyte, and even younger than she, judging by his thin fuzz on his chin.

He folded his hands. "You must seek the seventh son of the seventh son. He is of your blood, the missing component that will complete your circle. It is only with a complete circle that you will find the means to stand against your foes."

She closed her eyes. Though it wasn't clear if the acolyte knew the person's actual identity, his name came to Gwenwhyfar's mind instantly.

He raised his staff. "That is all."

"Thank you, wise ones." She bowed again, and returned her boat on the shore.

This trip had indeed given her both insight and answers. She understood that the incomplete circle was, of course, her incomplete family, torn apart by the blood feud that had lasted three generations.

The only seventh son of the seventh son she knew of was none other than Enri Loiol, her cousin, and the leader of the Euskaldunak.

She'd never met any of her grandmother's people, as the rift occurred long before her birth. Her father, Lord Erwan, witnessed it, a mere child of four. Even at that tender age, the events made a vivid impression upon him, and Tierney told her of their father's long nights of brooding over the situation in the great hall while nursing a bowl of cider.

As far as Gwenwhyfar knew, the Loiols and their tribe had not entered the war against Harappa. They tended to concern themselves solely with their own doings, and made little contact with outsiders aside from minimal trade. Their traditions were not unlike those of her own people, just not to the same extreme of isolationism.

Like their Breizhian cousins, the Euskaldunak prided themselves as impressive fighters, a people who knew how to find solutions with limited resources. They left Atlantis with the other exiles, though they were a distinct tribe from the Breizhians. Both tribes agreed upon only one point: that Atlantis had fallen into godlessness and decadence. Far better for them to forge their own destiny apart from the island superpower.

While she now had a solution, it led to a new problem.

She rowed across the narrow strait back to the continent. In regards to the wellbeing of her home, the idea of healing the rift was perfect. Perfect and simple— but not easy.

Most of all, she worried what price Enri would ask if he consented to help her.

"THE DRUIDS TOLD YOU to go groveling to Atlantis for food? And you gave them *an entire leg* from the hart for that useless 'advice'? I'm beginning to question their worth."

"Tierney!" Gwenwhyfar scolded. "Don't utter such blasphemy. That's *not* what they told me. Going to Atlantis was my idea, and I assure you, I have no intention of groveling. You know Mayor Werta doesn't stand upon such delusions."

Strapping and handsome despite his often harsh mien, Tierney found it difficult to articulate strong emotions, especially when it came to tenderness. "I don't like it. It's degrading the office of a regent."

"Nor do I, but I don't see that we have any other choice," she reasoned. "A mail ship arrived yesterday. They depart for Atlantis tomorrow. I will travel with them. This journey poses no hardship on our people."

"You will be away," he contended, "that is hardship enough. Our people look up to you. You are the heart of Ker-Ys. You give them hope better than Cahan or I can." In his worry, his sea blue eyes faded to a stormy gray, his contention the closest expression of love he felt capable of giving.

Gwenwhyfar regarded her older brother with empathy. "Then they will believe that I can bring them the things they need."

Tierney balled his fists, but he produced no further points with which to argue. "At least take Etxarte with you. I won't let you go alone."

She assented to his condition. "This brings me to what the Druids *did* say..."

He moved over to the table and poured a cup of mead, predicting that her next topic would take considerably longer than the first one.

"We must reconcile with the Euskaldunak if we are to survive this war," she said.

It was rather blunt, perhaps, but she knew Tierney hated it any time somebody did not come to come right to the point.

A line appeared between his brows. "Now you've truly lost your mind."

"Where else will we get the manpower to make up for our losses? They're the only ones who aren't involved in the war yet. If we don't secure their allegiance, someone else will, and *they* will benefit from the Euskaldunak's fresh resources."

"Resources?" he laughed dryly. "Their land doesn't exactly flow with rivers of milk and honey."

"But they've learned to use well what they do have. Not only are they surviving, they're thriving. Maybe they can't help us with supplies, but their warriors can defend our people. You know I'm not the first person to suggest this course."

"Cahan has proposed this idea as well," he admitted. "But will you do what's necessary to form this alliance? You ran away the last time we tried to make an alliance." His grip on his drinking bowl tightened. "What about your Roman paramour?"

She met his gaze head on, ignoring that last jab. "I'm older and wiser now. Besides, who says *I* have to be the one who's married off? It's my brothers' turn to step up this time." She kept her arms at her sides, so as not to appear defensive.

Tierney chewed his bottom lip, mulling over her suggestion. "I suppose that's fair."

"Since Cahan also thinks it a good plan, let *him* marry this time—"

"We'll decide that later," he interrupted. "You're forgetting the original dispute. Only a woman of grandfather's line can heal the rift, according to the ancient ways. Assuming Loiol will agree to make an exception, has he an eligible lady relative? What if he doesn't? And what if he insists on keeping to tradition?"

"As you said, we'll decide what to do depending on what the Euskaldunak say."

"Gwenwhyfar..." Tierney exhaled, not sure how to finish his thought. "You and your schemes."

He set down his drink, and paced from one side of the room to the next. "Very well, I'll humor your endeavor. But only on the condition that Cahan agrees, too."

"I wouldn't dream of making a match for him without his consent," she answered, trying her hardest to leave out any sarcasm.

My, how the tides have turned!

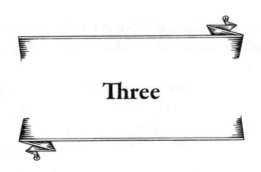

Three

GWENWHYFAR SAILED FOR Atlantis on the small mail ship, *Sea Harp*. Aside from a few bundles of correspondence, the ship had an empty hold. She intended to fill before she returned. But they needed more than supplies. Not even Atlantis could replace the population they had lost. She stared long and hard at the rolling waves, willing a solution to come to her mind.

After many hours of arguing, Cahan consented to marry one of Loiol's relatives for the sake of forging an alliance with the Euskaldunak. Though he'd done the same to her, Gwenwhyfar found herself incapable of gloating over the turning of tables. The more handsome and agreeable of her two brothers, Cahan likely had entertained hopes of falling in love, albeit he never voiced such sentiments.

But what would they do if a suitable female relative didn't exist? She couldn't possibly throw away her love for Marcus and marry Enri as her parents intended at her birth.

No I can't, she reiterated.

While gazing over the tossing waves, another incident from her family's history entered her mind. An ancestor of hers—she couldn't remember his name at the moment—once made an alliance with a Veneti leader without a marriage, as neither he nor his counterpart had an eligible female relative. To seal their agreement, they cut open their palms and grasped them until their blood ran together.

If only that was an option open to me, she thought sadly.

As a woman, she could only marry if she wished to form an alliance. What was more, most considered such alliances like that of her ancestor less desirable, given that they were less reliable. History ran rife with examples of failed alliances of that form, while few people felt inclined to go to war against their own kin. Or at least, everyone seemed to believe that method worked. Never mind that the exact occurrence came to pass between her grandfather and great uncle.

Her stomach rumbled.

"You need to eat." Etxarte walked up behind her.

Her guardian since her father's untimely death, the venerable Captain of the Guard and weapons master of Euskaldunak extraction served as the closest resemblance to a parent she'd known. Not only did she rely on his counsel in most matters, it was he who trained her the way of the sword.

"You're too skinny as it is, girl," he continued. "Build up your strength. You're going to need it."

She felt awful for enjoying a far better fare on the ship than anything her people had benefited from in many long, cold months. "You're right," she surrendered, consoling herself with her intention to return soon with supplies.

As she followed her guardian to the dining cabin, she caught sight of the captain on the command deck, staring out to sea with his hands clasped behind his back. She'd once observed Marcus standing in that same pensive posture.

If only the handsome Roman were of a more noble birth. Then she could simply marry him and reforge their earlier alliance with Rome. Alas, little if anything was ever that simple for her. Like Ker-Ys, Rome did not view a tribune of plebeian origins as a suitable candidate for representing the state in a foreign alliance.

She rubbed her eyes. An answer would come eventually. It must. The fear that said solution would end up not to her liking continued to lurk in the back of her mind.

MAYOR NEDRIL WERTA welcomed Gwenwhyfar to Atlantis with the same gusto and hospitality as he had on her first visit. A jovial fellow with curly, strawberry blond hair and green eyes, he never failed to bring a smile to her face. Most other politicians she'd met previously were oily and deceitful, but not Werta. The middle-aged Atlantean cared a great deal about his constituents and their wishes, and didn't shrink from putting their needs above his own. She liked him from the start.

"Young Tribune Duilius was just here for supplies two days ago," he informed her with a knowing wink. "He'll be crushed when he learns he missed you. I have a suspicion he's rather sweet on you. Just take heed not to crush his Roman pride, my dear."

She should not have expected Marcus to be there. The tiny wish manifested itself in her heart all the same, and it was she who felt crushed. She smiled at the mayor and tried to put aside her disappointment. "I'll keep that in mind."

"It's none of my business, I know," continued the mayor, "but I should really like to see you happy and married. Have you chosen a good-looking young prince yet?"

She kept her warning kind, yet firm. "Mayor."

"Yes, yes, I've said too much. But promise me that when you do marry, you'll invite Ezria and me to your wedding." He adjusted the wide lapels of his jacket as though already imagining the event on his schedule.

"Your names will head the top of the guest list," she assured him.

"Good, good." This satisfied him for the moment, and he proceeded next to her difficulty. "Now there's the little matter of Ker-Ys's need for supplies..." He interrupted her explanation with a raised hand. "You need not even ask. Consider it done. We'll have the

Sea Harp ready to bring you home by the time we've finished meeting with the other allies."

"Mayor, I—"

"No need to thank me, my dear," he interrupted a second time. "Consider it a gesture of Atlantis' good will toward her cousins."

GWENWHYFAR RESISTED the urge to visit the library on the first day. There would be an opportunity for that later. First, she needed to focus on the meeting with the other ally representatives.

Before the meeting, she decided it prudent to take a walk to calm her nerves. Other than Werta, the only other semi-friendly person in attendance would be Hamilcar Barca, adversary of Marcus' father during Rome's war with Carthage. Though he did not voice much opposition at their last encounter, she expected little approval from his corner of the table.

What unnerved her was when she spotted the name of another old acquaintance on the attendance scroll: Lucius Cornelius Scipio represented the interests of Rome this time.

Scipio. She hadn't heard his name in over six years. Yet she suspected that name would fill her with dread for as long as she lived. Anyone who dwelt in Rome knew him. He served a term with Marcus' father as consul.

Wandering the path along the canal, she saw a tavern ahead. A quick drink—just the thing to fortify her courage. Sure enough, the cheery music and atmosphere soon lightened her mood when she entered. The place was rather dark compared to the noon sunlight, though it seemed well-kept and respectable enough. One of the advantages Atlantis possessed was that any woman could walk the streets of the city without fear, though Werta warned her about a few of the hill settlements in the northwestern interior of the continent.

A lovely middle-aged woman with light brown hair and twinkling blue eyes stood at the bar to take her order. Right away, Gwenwhyfar warmed up to her. "What will you have, my lady?" the tavern keeper asked as she sat down at the bar.

"Wine. Without water."

She looked back in surprise. "That doesn't strike me as your usual poison. I thought a lady of your station would order mead. We brew our own here in Atlantis, you know."

"I'm not here for a casual drink," the princess admitted. "I'm on my way to a meeting."

"Ah," she said, reaching for a bottle underneath the counter. "The war council?"

Gwenwhyfar nodded. She knew many Atlantean officials had no qualms about frequenting the taverns of the city and rubbing elbows with their constituents. As long as she refrained from revealing any state secrets, conversing with a tavern keeper would do no harm.

"That's a tough crowd, I'll grant you that one." She poured some of the liquid into an elegant glass. "But I have good news for you. Werta is your greatest supporter, my lady. Here in Atlantis, that counts for a good deal. You just say what you want and he'll back you up."

"How do you know that?" Taking a sip, she savored the pleasant burn of the liqueur in her throat.

"He's my husband," she returned with obvious pride.

"Oh! You're Ezria?" exclaimed Gwenwhyfar. "He's a good man."

"Aye, he is," she said, her pretty smile growing wider. "Holler if you'd like another. But my guess is that one will be enough for your purposes." She busied herself with wiping up the contents of a spilled cup further down on the counter.

Gwenwhyfar's gaze traveled past Ezria to another customer sitting directly across from her. Upon catching his eye by accident, she offered a polite acknowledgment. He in turn raised his glass to her, and returned his attention to his drink.

Shahin, she remembered, the Persian tailor who sewed the exquisite golden gown she wore during her last visit.

What a mysterious character he was! "A shady fellow," Cahan had called him. Everyone else who spoke of him seemed to share her brother's opinion.

Reputation aside, his work was the finest Atlantis offered, and by far the most exceptional Gwenwhyfar had ever beheld. She couldn't help but wonder about him, his past, and how came to make his home in Atlantis.

A glance over at the dripping water clock told her the time had come to face her insecurities and perform the task before her. With a sigh, she paid her tab and left.

"Come back any time," Ezria called as she headed out the door.

UP TO THAT POINT, CAPTAIN Kenda Ptah had reclined in his chair, having unexpectedly joined the meeting of allies when his ship pulled into port ahead of schedule. Now, he reacted to the mounting tension in the room by leaning forward, like a lighthouse holding fast against a raging sea.

Gwenwhyfar resisted the urge to rise to her feet in exasperation.

Scipio had challenged every single point she brought to the table. The usual Roman habit of picking nits with any Carthaginian in sight forgotten, he decided instead to direct his criticisms toward her.

"We can hold our own against the enemy for the time being," she affirmed in a calm tone.

Scipio disagreed. "I question the abilities of Ker-Ys. Your navy, such as it was, is not yet rebuilt. And Rome cannot keep sending fleets to rescue you."

"I assure you, general," she reiterated through her teeth. "Our lines *will* hold."

Scipio knitted his brows. "How do you intend to garner the additional manpower to accomplish this feat? Your forces are spent."

"Not *all* spent," she pointed out. "Our coastguard patrols Breizhian waters."

Hamilcar Barca lazily waved a fly out of his face. "Let her alone already, Scipio. They're giving it their best. We can ask for no more."

"If Rome had settled for 'giving it our best' as you call it," he quipped, "we would not have defeated you."

"I have a plan," she said, projecting far more confidence than she felt.

Barca looked up in earnest for the first time in at least an hour, intending to retort, only to forget his come back when curiosity replaced animosity. "There, you see. She has a plan."

Scipio folded his arms. "Perhaps you'd care to share this plan with the rest of us."

From the wall behind her, she sensed Etxarte's restless movements. He stood with the other bodyguards and attendants. Outside of the gymnasium or sports arenas, Atlantis prohibited the carrying of weapons on municipal grounds. A wise precaution, even if her guardian's fingers itched without holding a sword or his preferred bow. Given his usual habits of outspokenness, it astonished her that he kept silent under Scipio's verbal attacks.

Werta's kind expression offered more encouragement. "Please do, Lady Gwenwhyfar. Perhaps we can give you additional suggestions?"

She focused her attention on the mayor, and away from Scipio's disapproving frown. "You may recall, from our mutual history, the Euskaldunak? A tribe that left Atlantis with my Breizhian ancestors three hundred years ago?"

"Of course," Werta said. "Every Atlantean is taught that event in school."

Ptah tapped his fingers on the table. "It was my understanding the Euskaldunak had all died out. The land they chose to settle on is harsh and inhospitable. Are some of them still around?"

"More than a mere few of them remain," Scipio reported. "We call them the Vascones. They allied with Carthage against us in the recent war. If you succeed in enlisting them, my lady, you will find invaluable fighters indeed," he conceded. "Only take heed, lest they turn against you."

Gwenwhyfar resisted the urge to react and give that cur the satisfaction that he'd gotten to her. "I think I can handle them, given they're my own kin."

Barca perked up again, his black beard prickling. "You mean you are part Vascone?"

"*Euskaldunak*," she corrected. "My bloodline is not as pure as some can boast, but yes."

The Carthaginian threw his head back and laughed.

Werta, Ptah, and the other Atlanteans likewise found the revelation amusing, allowing their amusement to show now that their counterpart had broken the ice. Only Scipio kept his mouth hardened into a thin line, his face a blank, unreadable mask.

"What's so funny?" she demanded, still feeling defensive.

Werta answered for them. "It explains a lot, my lady. In the best sense, of course. That is why you are so tenacious—why we *all*," he looked around the room to silence any opposition, "have faith that you will uphold your responsibilities to the other allies. We wish you the best of success in this endeavor."

She rose, taking the chance to aid him in bringing the long meeting to a close. "Thank you, mayor."

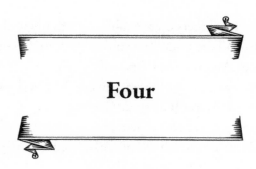

Four

THE MEETING NEARLY drove Kenda Ptah batty. He berated himself for attending when he might have skipped it on the pretense that his ship had pulled into harbor late. Nobody would have been the wiser. He didn't even change out of his salty armored uniform before rushing over there.

Stupid of me! The thought made him press his palm to his forehead.

Normally, he might have gone to Ezria's tavern after a ridiculous waste of time like that. But his curiosity outweighed his annoyance. What went on between Princess Gwenwhyfar and that Roman coot, Scipio?

True, he knew little about Gwenwhyfar's previous history in Rome. Whatever this issue was, it had to involve Marcus. Kenda *knew* that much. Otherwise, the girl would not have been so on edge around the general. He racked his brains trying to remember any connection Marcus might have mentioned in regards to Scipio, but to no avail.

One particular person, he felt certain, would know. But would said person feel inclined to surrender the story? That might take some doing.

He meandered into Shahin's shop.

The tailor looked up from his work, delighted to have a customer. "Ah, Captain. What can I get for you this lovely evening? Getting promoted again soon? I have just the material for a fine uniform any admiral would envy."

"Don't wish that upon me," Kenda warned, pushing the bolt aside.

The last time he entered the shop was when he required his captain's dress uniform. He would admit, he looked sharp arrayed in Shahin's handiwork. Proud as he felt that day, he held no aspirations for rising any higher in the ranks. His current responsibilities bore enough weight on his shoulders. This visit, he was in the market for something else entirely.

"No?" Shahin's smile turned wily. "You've finally found a mistress at last, then? A pretty dress for a pretty lady?"

Kenda straightened his back. "No. I've had my fill of women for one lifetime."

He returned his eyes to his work. "In my opinion, one lifetime is never enough. But that's not why you're here. You seek information."

Try as he might, he could never seem to outfox Shahin, who he long ago decided was the prince of foxes. *Light and darkness, I'm starting to sound like Marcus!* How could any honest man hope to pull the wool over a fox's eyes?

Kenda came right to it. "Didn't you tell me once that you worked in Rome as a gardener before you came here?"

"That's common enough knowledge. The Senate grounds looked better when I kept them than they ever had. Better than they look now, I'm told," the fox added with some gratification.

Obviously, Shahin did not intend to volunteer anything relevant on his own. He would have to ask for the specific answers he desired. "Did you know Marcus Duilius when you lived there?"

"I may have seen him in passing a few times. His father, Admiral Gaius, is better known. But you know the young tribune better than I ever could." He leaned forward to gage his machine's spacing between stitches.

"As a fellow warrior, yes. But even friends don't always share events of the past."

"You would know, wouldn't you?" Shahin looked up with narrowed eyes, rendering his appearance even more snake-like. "This isn't some kind of spy mission, is it? Because if it is, you've come to the wrong man. I'm not in that line of work anymore—I mean it."

Kenda doubted that, but did not contradict the claim aloud. "Of course not," he chuckled. "It's only curiosity about my old friend. Call it gossip, if you will. A distraction, to get my mind off of this infernal war." Inwardly, he groaned. *Now I sound like Werta.*

To his surprise, Shahin accepted the answer. "Well, that does make a difference. What do you want to know about him, then?"

"His attachment to Lady Gwenwhyfar—or rather Lady Varina, as she was known in Rome. When did it begin?" He wished he possessed more skill in the art of subtlety. Compared to Shahin, he was little better than a clucking old hen.

"What makes you think I would know anything about their relationship?" Shahin kept his gaze on his stitches.

Ah-ha! He *did* know something about it. Kenda barely caught that flicker of recognition on his face—but he'd caught it. "Because you were there."

"I can't really say..."

Liar. Aloud, he said, "You must have seen the attraction between them even then."

"Well, I suppose I may have noticed it when Duilius—he was only a centurion then —had some sort of debate with her in the garden on the Senate grounds."

"A conversation you overheard while hiding behind some bush, eh?" Kenda bared his teeth in a triumphant grin.

"I overheard a good many conversations as a gardener," the Persian admitted. "Quite by accident."

Kenda's mouth twitched. "Right."

"Criticize me all you wish," he returned coolly, "but remember that you come to me because of the very actions you denounce. Now, do you want to hear more, or are you going to stand there and pass judgment on me all day?"

"Alright, sorry," the captain surrendered. "Tell me more."

"Apparently, she stormed into the Senate moments earlier to rake Duilius' patron over the coals. Some sort of offense to her husband, one of the senators, who was absent at the time."

"And they let her in?"

Now it was Shahin's turn to smile. "Would you have tried to bar her way?"

Kenda considered the question. "I might have *tried*. But I imagine she might have managed to talk her way past even me if she wished."

"Exactly. This made quite the impression on Duilius. He's been infatuated with her ever since."

"He *is* infatuated with her," Kenda agreed. "He can hardly think straight when it comes to her."

The tailor tied off the last stitch. "There's more, if you're interested."

"I hoped there would be." Kenda pulled a chair over and sat down.

"Petronius' family blamed her for his murder, as you've heard, but someone mentioned to me—I can't say who, secrets of the trade, you know—that it was someone else who did him in."

"Of course someone else did him in," said Kenda. "Does that slip of a girl look like a murderess to you?"

"Never trust appearances," Shahin countered. "Or, so Petronius' family claimed."

"Ugh, what idiots! They were just using her as a scapegoat." He thought a moment. "Surely Marcus didn't believe that about her?"

Shahin's black eyebrows climbed to his hairline. "What do you think?"

"He didn't. In fact, I'm surprised he stood by and allowed..." He looked back to the tailor for confirmation of his guess.

"The next thing I heard, the body of Duilius' superior was seen floating down the Tiber." He held up his handful of bobbins in a shrug.

Kenda whistled. "That's how he got promoted so quickly. And all this time I thought it was solely on account of his achievements in battle."

"It *is* a common enough method for climbing the ranks in the Roman military." He rose and went over to the window. "Well, well. Don't look yet, captain, but our lady in question just passed by. She's headed to Ezria's tavern."

"I wonder if she knows?"

"Your guess is as good as mine in this instance."

"Hmm." Kenda suspected that was the first truthful statement Shahin had uttered since he stepped into his shop. "Where does Scipio fit into all of this?"

"That's the easy piece of the puzzle." Shahin looked him right in the eye. "The wife of Duilius' superior was Scipio's daughter."

"His *daughter*?"

Shahin nodded. "She disappeared around the same time. Most believe she shared her husband's fate. I expect Scipio thinks that as well."

Kenda realized his mouth hung open. He closed it. "Does it get any worse?"

"All of that happened around the time I left, so I couldn't say." He looked over at the waterclock. "My, look at the time. Closing hour already."

Kenda knew how to take a hint. He also knew he would get nothing further out of the Persian that evening. He hovered in the doorway. "Thanks, Shahin," he said before dashing out to the street.

"My pleasure, captain," he called after him. "Nothing like gossip to pass the afternoon, eh?"

But the Nubian didn't stay to respond. As he made his way down the street, he considered ducking his head into Ezria's to see if Gwenwhyfar was still there. But he decided against the notion. He felt he'd already violated her privacy enough for one day by gossiping with Shahin.

Of course, the possibility remained that the tailor had made up the entire story.

No, he decided. Fact often proved stranger than fiction. It was all too horrible for somebody to simply dream up. A lucky thing for both Marcus and Gwenwhyfar that a truce stayed Scipio's hand from carrying out his vengeance.

THE NEXT THING SHE knew, Gwenwhyfar found herself back in Ezria's Tavern on the Canal.

She plopped herself down on the chair. "Better give me a bigger glass."

Ezria's sparkling blue eyes widened. "That bad, eh? Didn't my husband do right by you?"

"Oh, he tried. But an 'old friend' countered anything and everything I had to say. Why can't these people rise above this pettiness, at least for the sake of our common predicament?" She knew should not talk this much, even if Werta would tell his wife about the matter anyway.

Ezria poured wine into a tall glass. "You'd think they would. But mark my words, the jackal did it because he saw something in you that's lacking in himself. That's why people act like that, you know."

"I had not thought of that." Gwenwhyfar caught herself before letting any more slip. Best to keep her past life where it belonged: in the past. The bartender raised a brow, fishing for information. A politician like Werta was wise to marry a tavern keeper. Only the gods could guess at all that Ezria heard, or could place herself in a position to hear.

Gwenwhyfar returned a polite smile, indicating the subject had closed. "Thank you."

One of the waiters hovered behind Ezria before she got the chance to throw her line back out. "Hey, uh, boss..." he stuttered.

She didn't turn to face him, but closed her eyes in annoyance. "Words. Use them."

"...the lady at table twelve isn't happy."

"What's wrong?" "The wine isn't red enough."

That made her turn. "*What?*" Throwing down the rag, she went over to tend to her customer. "I'll be right back."

But Gwenwhyfar no longer wished for conversation. She wanted to sit and think with her glass of wine. Picking up her drink, she made her way over to a table in a deserted corner for more privacy.

Coming here was a bad idea, she decided. She felt confident no actual harm had been done, but her mind reeled at what she might have let slip, had she allowed her control to loosen further. She would take this second drink with more caution, then leave the tavern before she made a disaster out of the evening.

No sooner than she took the first sip when none other than Lucius Scipio strolled through the door. She tried to lean backwards into the shadow of the corner, but it was too late. He'd already spotted her.

At least he'll stay on the other side of the room. To her horror, she found herself mistaken. Upon ordering his drink, he approached her table.

She cursed under her breath. "What do you want?" She surprised even herself with the venom in her tone.

It didn't deter him. "To talk to you."

"You said quite enough earlier," she shot back.

"I merely voiced concerns anyone else in my position would have. I didn't get elected consul for nothing, you know. May I sit down?"

She shrugged. "Something tells me you'll do so no matter what I say."

He patiently remained standing.

"Fine," she snapped. "State your business and be done with it." The alcohol swam in her head, but she intended to leave soon enough.

Cool and collected, he took the chair across from her. "I'm curious about you." She raised a sarcastic brow. Scipio's patrician façade cracked at last. "You *are* modest. All this time I thought those who reported this trait to me had merely succumbed to your feminine charms."

Now she did roll her eyes. "What do you care about that?"

He stared at her for several seconds. The man had an uncanny ability to make people feel small and insecure. "I didn't kill your husband."

Gwenwhyfar was taken aback. "Do you expect me to believe you had nothing to do with it?"

"No." He swirled the liquid around in his cup. "But it is the truth. Whether or not you chose to believe it is your own affair."

"Why tell me this now? Conscience interrupting your good night's sleep?"

He smiled thinly. "You assume I don't have a conscience. I suppose I can't blame you." He threw back the contents of his glass.

She grew more and more uncomfortable. If he didn't come to the point soon, she intended to get up and leave. Not for a second did she buy this pond sludge he tried to peddle to her. At the same time, she did wonder what he could possibly want with her. "Is that all you have to say?"

"Did you love Petronius?"

"You are a bold one." She realized he was in dead earnest. Something about him made her question her current opinion of him. "I hardly knew him. Given time, I think I could have. But that chance was taken away from me. And before you ask, the answer is no, I didn't kill your daughter."

The corners of his eyes crinkled. "I believe you." The unspoken statement, that he'd only moments before given her the same assurance and she didn't believe him, hung over them like a foreboding fog.

He signaled the waiter for two more drinks.

She almost pointed out to him that he hadn't *asked* her if she wanted another drink, but she stopped herself. She found that now, she was equally curious about him.

"Had I known about my daughter and Secundus' plot, I would have advised against it. It was ill-timed and poorly planned." Regret filled his voice.

She noted that he left "immoral" and "cowardly" out of his objections.

The drinks arrived. She left hers untouched on the table in front of her.

He took a sip. "It's no surprise the deed was traced back to them and retaliation ensued."

"I already told you I didn't do it. You're wasting your time looking for answers from me."

His steel gray eyes darted back upward to study her. "You don't know who did it?"

"The only person I can think of was in prison at the time."

Now his boring gaze intensified. "Even you aren't that naïve. You know who did it, and you know why. He did it for you. Because he's enamored with you."

Gwenwhyfar met his hard stare. Though she had long suspected Marcus's part in the deed, he never confessed it to her. "And now you're going to kill him, aren't you? Is that what you came to tell me?"

Having obtained what he came for, Scipio rose from his chair. "I'm not a cruel man, my lady. I once loved a woman the way Duilius loves you. I would have done anything for her, even killed. But in the end, Drusilla's mother betrayed me for another man. Fortunately, I was still young enough that it didn't destroy my career or my family honor."

"What will you do?" she demanded.

"Now that I've met you and learned you are everything my wife was not...?"

She broke contact and instead looked into her still full glass. She found it impossible to keep up her front against this man. Her eyes watered as she waited for him to speak the words she so dreaded.

"Nothing," he finished. "I wish you well, Lady Gwenwhyfar." He paid for the drinks and left.

It was plain that Scipio admired his enemy's audacity. Another man (perhaps himself?) might have satisfied his honor by commissioning a *defixio*, and waiting for the gods to wreak vengeance upon his enemies.

But not Duilius. Like his father, he did not wait around for deities to fulfill his aspirations, but like a true Roman took the reins of life and shaped the course of his own destiny.

Though she hadn't planned to accept the drink Scipio bought for her, she grabbed it anyway and left for her accommodations. To outward appearances, she felt confident she gave the impression of perfect control.

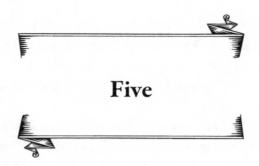

Five

GWENWHYFAR ALWAYS FOUND refuge and peace in libraries. The library at Atlantis proved no exception. Despite her unpleasant encounter the previous evening, she found herself in a better mood the next morning.

"I should have come here first," she sighed.

She reveled in the smell of dusty old papyrus, recalling with amusement her first time smelling it as a girl. She found it stuffy then, but now it conjured up wonderful memories of learning about the wide world, the wise words of philosophers that plowed the depths of the human heart and soul, and of and epic stories that sent her heart racing.

As was the case each time she had entered this particular library, her mind whirled with choices. What should she read first? Given the current state of the world, it would behoove her to learn more about the peoples of the Far East, she decided.

The librarians would know how much knowledge had been gathered on the subject, and she wondered if they knew about every single scroll they cared for, as suggested by the all-knowing demeanor they projected. *Surely not*, she chuckled to herself.

Upon inquiry, she was guided to a lonely corner on the uppermost level. "You may summon me if you require anything else, my lady," said the librarian's monotone assistant. "I am Atticus."

She thanked him, and delved into a shelf of scrolls. Spreading the first one onto a reading table, she unrolled a work on the spiritual beliefs of the Hindu, a religion in the Far East. That in turn led to an account of the Followers of Erykanis, an order of scientists, scholars, and philosophers, who mathematically predicted the destruction of Atlantis.

When met with persecution, they departed and established their order in Alexandria. Not only do they preserve knowledge and the culture of Atlantis, they take it upon themselves to combat the forces of the Otherworlds. Their symbol is the trident, or the Greek letter Ψ. The trident is likewise their weapon of choice, in keeping with their Atlantean origins.

After some time passed, she heard a low hum behind her. Kenda Ptah leaned over her shoulder to have a look. "What are you reading today?"

"Captain," she returned with a warm smile. "How nice to run into you here."

He inclined his head to her. "Who would have thought a slip of a girl would have a mind filled with knowledge? No wonder you throw Marcus' world into chaos."

"I've been educated as a leader to my people," she answered modestly, though his compliment pleased her. She tilted the open scroll toward him. "What do you know of the Followers of Erykanis? It says they remain an active order of scholars in Alexandria. The philosopher Solon was one of them, apparently."

"Humph! That explains where Plato got his outlandish ideas."

"You don't approve of them," she observed. "Aside from their political views, why?"

"Because they're fanatics who twist reason to make their conspiracies sound true. They actually want us to believe they count *mermages* among their numbers—of all things!"

Gwenwhyfar kept silent. She remembered what little Finn had told her of his incarceration in the sea farms, where he'd met people who inherited the ability to dive deep beneath the sea, to depths that would spell the death of any normal person.

True enough, the tales that reported the mages of the sea using pools of water as gateways between different locations sounded incredible. The Druids, at least, accepted that water connected the real world to Other realms.

"You don't believe in *mermages*, do you?"

"I don't know. My people tell many stories of the *morghens*, as we call them."

He held up a single finger. "Ah, but have you seen one of them for yourself? With your own eyes?"

"No," she conceded, "but neither have I seen the Library at Alexandria. Until I travel there myself, I must rely upon what others tell me about it."

"Not every person's testimony is accurate," he persisted.

"Fair enough. That doesn't discount what a person experiences, just because he lacks the abilities to describe it."

Ptah laughed. "I'll not argue any longer with you, girl. Instead, I propose we investigate that passageway we discovered last time.

"Oh? I was going to ask if you learned anything else on our common subject of interest."

"I have. Not from here, though." He gestured, meaning the tight-lipped staff. "My travels and talks with others have yielded information."

She whispered in spite of her mounting excitement. "Do you think it's really a passage?"

His lips turned up slightly and a devious look gleamed in his eye. "Let's find out."

An odd sense of foreboding came over her, yet it could not suppress the overwhelming curiosity Ptah's proposition had awakened. "And if we're stopped again?"

"Better to beg forgiveness again than ask permission we surely won't get. Besides, with this smile, I can get away with anything." He flashed his pearly whites to demonstrate.

They walked together back down the stairs, toward the back part of the library. They held their scrolls in their arms, feigning a search for a vacant reading table. None of the other patrons took notice of them, nor did any of the library staff.

"What did Werta say when you asked him about it?" she whispered.

"He said I was overreacting, and that the librarians are all eccentrics who don't get out much. He claims I'm completely free to go and see the back rooms, though he didn't think I'd find anything worth writing about to my relatives in Nubia."

"I don't know." She bit her lip. "He didn't see the look on that woman's face. But I agree with him the librarians are eccentric."

When they reached the shelf in question, it appeared as before: an ordinary ledge for books.

Handing her his armful of scrolls, Ptah felt around the edges of the shelf. "It was...here, as I recall. Yes, I can feel the lever."

She turned to glance around for anyone who might have been watching them. The coast clear, and she nodded for him to continue.

He drew in a deep, thrilled breath, and pulled the lever.

The shelf inched forward on its own accord. "We were right!" He pulled the shelf back the rest of the way, revealing a tunnel carved out of rough stone. "Ladies first," he said. "I'll pull the shelf back in place behind us."

There was no time to lose. She set down her bundle and crept through the opening before some passerby saw them.

Candle sconces on the walls lit the passageway. Even with their light, it took her eyes a few moments to adjust to the dimness once Ptah closed the entrance. When her vision cleared, she saw not one, but many passageways, leading in all directions.

"Which way?" she asked.

He pointed straight ahead. "This way is as good as any. But remember which way we came. I don't care to spend the rest of my life wandering this maze waiting for some Minotaur to eat us. At least you'd taste sweeter, which will draw the monster away from me," he added with a grin.

"How reassuring." She walked on, listening for other footsteps.

The corridor seemed empty.

A shiver trembled down her back. She could easily picture a monster like the Minotaur lurking through these corridors. *Stop it!* she chided herself.

They passed by a doorway, which opened up into a storehouse rather than another corridor. The chamber was as large as any one of the levels in the public section of the library, though it felt centuries older.

"Want to look in here?" he asked.

"You read my mind. To think, all of this lay beneath our feet, and we didn't know it!" she breathed. "Why do you suppose this place is kept secret?"

He ground his teeth, though his voice remained calm. "Your guess is as good as mine, girl. I didn't know my adopted people were this secretive. Openness is an aspect Atlanteans usually prize."

After another quick look down the corridor to make sure they were indeed alone, they approached the first shelf. She chose a scroll, then unrolled it on one of the reading tables. The writing looked familiar, though she could not translate it. What she *did* recognize, was the Ψ symbol of the Followers of Erykanis.

"It looks like a prophecy," Ptah supplied, answering her unspoken question. "In the ancient language of the Atlanteans. Every child learns it in school, but we don't speak it any longer since Greek is far more useful." He studied the text. "I came here as an adult, so my proficiency is a bit rusty."

"Can you translate it?"

"Hmm. I think so. Bring it closer to the light..." He examined it for a few minutes in front of the candle, then read:

A mighty people rises from obscurity.

The world unites together.

A great civilization destroyed.

The savior of men comes at long last.

"The prophecy of Delphi's oracle," she realized. "How?"

"She must have heard it from somewhere else. I've said for years that's all nothing but smoke and mirrors, designed to keep people in servitude. But few listen." He stopped himself from continuing on his usual rant.

He turned back to the text:

A seventh son of a seventh son holds the key.

He must complete the circle together with

A woman who will save a doomed kingdom.

She gasped. "The Druid priests spoke those words to me the day before my journey here!"

The captain remained skeptical. "You already know what I think about that."

"But it doesn't make sense," she insisted. "They write down only the prayers for rituals. Most of them cannot even read. I don't see how they could have known about this."

Ptah shrugged, and read the final stanza.

The children of Blood Seek to destroy the world.

Peoples of all lands must band together.

An island sinks beneath the depths.

"While this is interesting," he said, "I don't believe in such nonsense. This is obviously a work from our superstitious past. See the date here? That it *appears* to have bearing on today is coincidence, nothing more."

She allowed him have his last word, deciding it best not let on how much this all unnerved her. The text influencing the oracle's prophecy she could entertain temporarily, for argument's sake.

But that second part?

No, she could not convince herself that the Druids already knew about this ancient writing.

"Let's explore the rest of this maze," Ptah suggested. "I don't want to spend all of my time here on a single scroll written by a band of fanatics."

Gwenwhyfar agreed that they should continue onward. They moved on down the corridor to the next chamber, where consoles with hundreds of buttons spread out before them.

"Amazing!" she marveled. "Just when I think I've been out-wondered, Atlantis surprises me yet again. What do they all do?"

"I'm a navigator, not a scientist," he reminded her. "But I will say this: I intend to pay another visit to Werta."

She slowly nodded. "Somehow, I have the feeling he may not know about all of this."

"He had better *not*," he warned.

They continued on through the corridor to the next chamber, somewhat smaller than the first, which held more shelves of dusty scrolls.

"How many rooms do you suppose there are?" she inquired.

"I have no idea," he answered. "But feel free to wager—"

"Ah-hem!" cleared a throat behind them.

They both started.

The Head Librarian loomed in front of them, a warning glare in her eyes. "I warned you this area is restricted," she scolded.

Her height, coupled with Gwenwhyfar's guilt at being caught made the woman look all the more formidable.

"We were just..." she stammered.

"Leave immediately," the librarian interrupted. "Captain Ptah, Mayor Werta has sent a summons for you. It's waiting for you at the front desk."

KENDA ENTERED THE MAYOR's posh office in complete bewilderment.

Of course, he'd intended to storm into the room and demand answers, but he did not expect Werta to summon him first. Either he had done something wrong—and he was certain he had not; sneaking into the staff area of the library hardly warranted the mayor's attention—or he was about to get promoted.

Werta looked up when he entered, his tone was all business. "This meeting is classified."

"I understand." Perhaps this *did* have something to do with the secret maze in the library? They had stumbled upon a control room of sorts, after all.

"You're being sent on a secret mission," said Werta. "To Pataliputra, in India. You are to re-establish communication with King Ashoka, and learn all you can from him about the Harappans. The Council has promoted you to the position of Ambassador, with all the rights and privileges. Effective immediately."

Kenda blinked. He had run through a handful of the most likely scenarios that he thought would transpire during this meeting on his way from the library. This was not one of them. Not by a long shot.

"Why me?" he asked, once he recovered from his surprise.

"Who else? You're our resident expert on the Harappans by default. Or at least, our only military operative with firsthand experience and knowledge about them. Oh, there are plenty of academics," he snorted. "But we both know they wouldn't last the voyage over there." He handed Kenda a scroll of instructions.

"This is your doing, isn't it?"

"I convinced the Council to appoint you, yes. We need you, Kenda. *I* need you."

Kenda walked over to stare into the gentle waterfall of Werta's fish pond before opening his orders. "I won't even ask if this is voluntary."

"Good." Werta continued. "We've assigned a civilian who will go with you as your guide. Your packet there has all the information you need to know. Memorize it, then destroy it."

Kenda read through the orders.

The water clock on the desk dripped, reminding him of the passing seconds. Werta sat in patient silence. When he saw the identity of his partner, his jaw dropped.

He looked up at Werta. "You have *got* to be joking."

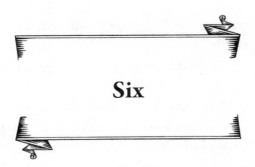

Six

IT WAS IRONY AT ITS finest that Shahin found himself closing up his shop just when his business reached its highest boom.

With the current state of affairs and the threat of war looming over them, the people of Atlantis grew more agitated by the day, sometimes by the hour. They flocked to their stores in search of material things to distract themselves from the harshness of reality. When the placebo wore off, back to the shops they went.

Yet Shahin experienced little regret at having to put a damper on his new found success. He never dreamed he'd admit it, but he grew weary of his lot as a spy. He was tired of the violence, tired of the constant deception, to the point where he wondered if he told the truth even to himself anymore.

Constantly, he moved around, never staying in one place long enough to grow lax. He trusted no one— unless the person was dead, and even then, he'd insist on first examining the person's body for himself before turning his back.

This was his chance to turn over a new leaf. Maybe, just maybe, he could stop running after this mission. A long shot—the actions and choices of his life up to then had grown into a shrieking kraken that haunted him each night. His ledger dripped with innocent blood. One stroke could not wipe all of it away at once.

But adding the first weight to the opposite side of the scale? He'd give that a whirl. What did he have to lose by this point? His life?

Lives were overrated in his line of work—his *former* line of work, he corrected himself.

A customer wandered into his shop. He should have locked the doors sooner.

"I'm about to close shop." He stopped when he saw the man.

He was a middle-aged Roman, a sailor, and of high rank by the looks of him. "I won't be long."

Shahin's curiosity was piqued. He recognized the Roman, though he couldn't recall his identity. Not surprising. He knew many Romans.

Old habits died hard, and the snoop part of him couldn't resist studying the fly that had sauntered into his net. Given his recent change in profession, he meant to let the fly go instead of eat him. No harm would be done. The salty Roman fingered a fine bolt of lavender silk.

"That fabric will cost a pretty denarius," said Shahin, though this customer could afford it. He looked up.

"For the right woman, it's well worth it."

"I see you have a schooled eye. Tell me more about this woman."

He dropped the silk. "She died long ago."

An uneasy familiarity manifested in Shahin's mind. Yes, he *had* met this Roman before. He was certain of that now.

"Tell me, Persian, where might one buy some of the *laaleh* flowers from your native land?"

Shahin sensed that the situation grew more precarious with the stranger's every word. "The *laaleh* is a demanding plant from what I'm told," he answered cautiously. "It doesn't grow outside of Persia, not even here in Atlantis."

"Ah, but I knew of a Persian gardener who successfully cultivated them in Rome. On the Senate building grounds, I believe it was." His eyes sharpened.

Now Shahin remembered the man's identity: Lucius Cornelius Scipio, of a powerful family virtually as old as Rome itself. Not a former customer, but...

"He must have possessed quite a talent for horticulture," Shahin said, refusing to be baited.

"He did. Among other things." He turned his attention to another bolt of cloth. "In fact, several high-ranking officials and personages met with most unnatural deaths around the same time of his tenure. Some are of the opinion that he had a hand in them."

So, he suspected. Shahin kept his features schooled. "Hearing a harrowing account like that makes me relieved those matters don't concern a plain and simple tailor such as myself."

Scipio glanced up again. "That's fortunate for you. You see, my daughter and her husband were among the victims. If I ever find the man who murdered them, it will not go well for him." He loomed closer, gritting his teeth. "He'll rue the day he was born."

"How do you know it wasn't a woman?" he quipped.

That threw the bloodhound off the scent temporarily. "Alright, I don't," the Roman conceded. "But one day, I'll know for certain and have my revenge."

"Such is the fate of one who choses that line of work. What," he inquired, trying to change the subject, "in the way of fabric were you looking for today, sir?"

Scipio drew himself up. "I'll buy nothing today. My wife and daughter are gone. And I'm not an effeminate milksop who wears soft clothing and stuffs himself with sugary dainties."

He turned to leave, but stopped in the doorway. His smile barely concealed the deadly fervor of his resolve. "Thank you for your insight. I may return another day, should I ever decide to take a mistress. Perhaps it may be as soon as tomorrow, hmm?" Bidding him a good afternoon, he departed.

Shahin permitted himself to relax. What a solace that he would travel far from Atlantis tomorrow.

In case Scipio intended to carry through with his threat, he decided to forgo packing away his merchandise and close up immediately.

Atlantis had not reached the point of social unrest, so looting wouldn't pose a problem as of yet. If or when it came to that, Shahin will have long returned to move his stock to a more secure location.

Provided he wasn't killed during the mission.

He shrugged. Should that end up the case, he wouldn't care anyway.

To occupy his racing mind, he ran through the possible explanations he would leave for his customers. "Let's see now. 'I've had a death in my family'? Effective, but too morbid for this current atmosphere. 'Gone on vacation'? No. That would arouse jealousy. Bad for business in these times."

Then he smiled. "'Gone fishing.' I've always wanted to use that."

With a chuckle, he picked up the door sign and wrote those words.

KENDA ROSE TO HIS FEET. "I wouldn't trust that man as far as I can throw him!"

Werta folded his hands together. "Nevertheless, you must work with him. Shahin is the most knowledgeable person we have, military or civilian. Believe me, I'd assign someone else to you if I could. There is no one else with better information on India and the Far East."

"Why do you need me, then?" He threw his hands in the air.

"Because I can trust you. I *don't* trust Shahin. But I don't doubt for a second that you will return with the information we need."

He crossed his arms and set his jaw, trying his hardest not to let slip the anger boiling inside him. "I suppose that means I'm in, seeing as I have little choice."

Werta smiled with relief, but he didn't deny the new ambassador's assessment. "Thanks, Kenda. I knew Atlantis can count on you."

"Yes, yes." He snapped his scroll into a fold without even bothering to roll it up, then stormed out of the office.

This was beyond stupidity! Gossiping with that Persian spy to pass the time was one thing. True, that morning he exchanged both that and information on Roman politics with the man. But if Werta and the Council simply assumed he'd put his life into the hands of that sneaky rat—and that's exactly what they had just done —they had another thing coming.

It's easy enough for them to tell me to stick my neck out! He doubted they would have gambled on such unrealistic speculations with their own hides.

"Idiots! How in Hades did they get elected? I don't recall voting for a single one of those booby birds, now that I consider it."

Turning down the assignment wasn't an option, that much was clear. *'All the rights and privileges,' eh?* Well, he intended to use that to his full advantage. Anything could happen on an ocean voyage, after all.

He intended to sleep with one eye open and a dagger under his pillow. If Shahin tried to pull any stunts, well it would be just too bad for him, wouldn't it?

The only thing stopping him from taking care of business right then and there was the matter of his ignorance about the languages and customs of India and the Far East. The mayor was correct about that. Officials there would have a knowledge of Greek, but that wouldn't help him much with traveling, observing the locals, listening in on conversations, or whatever else required for him to complete the mission.

"That dirty rat is luckier than he realizes." Or maybe he *did* realize it, and milked it for all it was worth?

Kenda stomped over to his apartment in order to finish reading the confounded piece of trash he held crumpled in his hand.

THE *Sea Harp* bobbed on the waves, loaded with supplies for Ker-Ys. A fresh, wind from the west captured her sails to bear them on their journey home.

"It's about time we left that blasted island," complained Etxarte. "That place unnerves me."

"I would have liked to spend more time at the library," said Gwenwhyfar. "But all the same, I'm happy to at least head in the direction home once more."

He leaned on the railing and studied her face. "Are you sure you know what you're doing?"

"No," she confessed. "But can you offer an alternative?"

He could not. "The Euskaldunak are our last hope. You know, I always had the feeling you would be the one to heal the rift. Others had said Cahan was the one, but I knew better."

"Given more time, he might have. He's usually better about burying the hatchet than I am." She felt her anxiety over the situation mount with each passing minute.

"I approve of this plan," Etxarte said, "because it's better than if Cahan were to try. I know it's not going to be easy for you."

"I will manage," she assured him.

Her guardian offered a warm smile. "I'm proud of you, my girl. You've grown up."

FOUR UNEVENTFUL DAYS out, and the *Sea Harp* crew bid farewell their escort ship just as she turned back for Atlantis.

Gwenwhyfar hated to see them go. One could never tell what they might encounter on the open waters during a war.

Though a supply *barca* carried much importance in these times, Atlantis could spare none of her warship to take them all the way back home. But Werta had assured her the Atlantean patrols policed the waters meticulously. Roman, Carthaginian, and sometimes the Mayan warships likewise frequented the area. They would not find themselves left alone for any extended periods of time.

But after their escort drifted out of sight, they did not encounter another vessel. Fair weather continued to favor their voyage, and the crew delighted at the sight of another crimson sunset.

Gwenwhyfar stared at the ceiling as she lay in her hammock. Moonlight shone into her cabin through a tiny window behind her. She rocked to the rhythm of the gentle waves, brooding.

My life is over, she thought. If only Marcus would somehow sail back into her life in with his powerful trireme and rescue her from her own determined schemes!

She pushed the wish away. A foolish dream, conjured up by her treacherous heart to steer her away from serving her people—her true destiny.

"A destiny of pining away from something I can never have?" she whispered to the darkness. "What kind of future is that?" The plank boards above her creaked, but otherwise did not answer her. "Would that I never had a heart to torture me!" After some time, she fell into a shallow, restless sleep.

To her dismay, she dreamed of Marcus.

SHE AWOKE WHEN DAWN broke. But it wasn't the light that roused her. Up on deck, the sailors yelled and scrambled to their posts.

Peeking out of her porthole, she discovered the cause for all that excitement. "Goddess help us!"

A Harappan raider loomed on the horizon. Even from that distance, she could hear the enemy's chanting, their sorceress egging them on in the chase of their prey. Her robes flowed with the wind, as she stretched her out her arms toward the churning sea. Angry clouds whirled above in a menacing sky.

"Kali! Kali!" Their invocations traveled over the waves to strike terror into the bosoms of their victims.

The horribly familiar waterspout dipped down from the clouds to touch the water in front of them.

She raced for the upper deck. Gripping the wooden ladder, she held on tight as the *Sea Harp* rocked and rolled on the rough waves.

"Hard to port!" she heard the first mate cry. "All hands: hold fast!"

The *barca* veered a sharp left, barely missing the whirling vortex.

Gwenwhyfar lost her grip on the ladder, and fell back down the ladder to her cabin deck. Fortunately, she didn't fall far.

After the ship finally righted, she managed to make her way up top, where Etxarte stood next to the captain. "They appeared right at dawn," her guardian yelled over the howling wind. "First mate says they've probably prowled these waters up and down for some time in search for targets."

"It's a wonder they missed us on the way over," added the captain. He held on to the railing as the vortex pulled on the *Sea Harp*.

"What of the patrols?" she asked.

Etxarte's lips thinned. "I think we can guess what happened to them."

"One warship against another, and you have an even chance, even against the Harappans," explained the captain. "They like to gang up on a lone target," he drew a finger across his neck, "and that's it for a single patrol ship."

"Lookout says he thinks he saw a pack of 'em in the early light, sailing south," Etxarte added. "This one broke off to chase us." Gwenwhyfar stared at the churning waterspout, wondering about what sort of heinous bargain their enemies must have made with their deities to wield such power. She imagined most sensible people wouldn't deem the sacrifice worth it. But they all knew the Harappans were not sensible people.

"Better get back below, my lady," urged the captain. "We're almost in firing range."

A nearby splash just off the bow added emphasis to his warning. Angry steam steam sizzled from where the fiery ball hit the water.

"Go on," Etxarte ordered, with a look that she'd known from childhood permitted no argument.

Disheartened, she went back to her cabin. Once inside, she bolted the door and drew her sword. If the Harappans forced their way in, they would find quite the surprise waiting for them.

She drew in deep, controlled breaths. Two seasons had passed since she last saw battle. In truth, terror filled her. She would face the bloodthirsty Harappans in combat again, and this time, her bodyguard wasn't there to look after her. Not that her guardian didn't intend to protect her—quite the contrary. He would not shrink from giving his life for her if it came to it.

But he'd already be dead by the time she went up against the boarders—that was the only way they'd reach her cabin in the first place.

She mustered up her courage, resolved to keep its fire burning within her for as long as necessary. Her thoughts turned to Marcus. *I wish I could have seen him one last time.*

Marcus would support Etxarte's view. "I can't fight if I'm worried about you getting hurt," she pictured him saying. "Don't worry, my Gwenwhyfar, I'll protect you!"

But those dismal thoughts deserved no place in her mind if she intended to stand with courage when her enemies burst through the door.

It moved her that Marcus and her guardian treasured her so, that they loved her enough to die defending her. She knew full well that the majority of men did not view her sex with the same high esteem.

At the same time, it seemed impractical for them to lock her away to wait while they fought, only for her to die anyway after they fell, with no man to defend her. No, she must rely on herself.

Ironic that Etxarte used the exact argument when convincing Tierney to allow him to teach her the ways of the sword. At least during the siege at Ker-Ys they'd come up with the halfway decent excuse that they needed her to protect those who could not defend themselves.

Now she must battle her own fears, listening on while her guardian and the men above were slain, and then wait to fight a second battle against the enemies— alone. The hope always remained fro them to win the day. She prayed for that. But a mail ship's crew against a Harappan war galley? Not a likely victory.

She entertained the idea of disobeying Etxarte and charging out anyway. Then she remembered the faces of the two good men who'd already died because she'd acted on her first impulse. "Ugh! This is maddening!" She stomped her foot, tempted to risk dulling the edge of her sword against the wood in her cabin.

Good. She was angry. Far better to feel anger than fear. Most warriors confessed that the fear never went away. They simply learned to better control it with experience. Given the choice, she preferred to avoid combat altogether.

"At least I don't have to go through with my earlier plan." Instead, it seemed she soon would meet her end. "I will make it such an end!" she vowed, flattening her palm against the blade of her sword.

"Repel boarders!" shouted the captain. The crew's battle cried followed his command.

An army of footsteps pounded above her. The fight had begun. Not that it would be much of a fight against a warship of ruthless villains and cutthroats. She hated just waiting there, unable to see what happened outside and above! From the tips of her toes, she glanced again out of her tiny window. The sea boiled around them.

Why didn't the Harappans simply blow them out of the water? Did they want prisoners? Her stomach tightened at the thought. All too well did she remember her own harrowing experience as their captive.

"Roman trireme!" she heard one of the officers exclaim. "To the south on the horizon!"

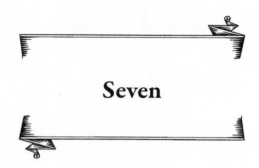

Seven

IT WAS AS THOUGH HER wish had manifested itself at her bidding.

Who am I fooling? Marcus isn't the only Roman captain sailing the seas these days. She sank to the floor, resting against the wall. Her tiny porthole afforded little in the way of a decent view. She must wait and hope for the best.

Time dragged on while the battle raged above her. Shots directed at their ship became less frequent, as the arrival of a trireme on the scene gave the enemy a more formidable target. The Romans would give them a run for their money, at least. Judging by the cheers of the crew, the new arrivals gave the Harappans quite the fight.

She heard some of the deck hands placing wagers. Why not? But if they lost, somebody would get cheated.

She sighed again, and began to recite poems to ward off the anxiety. "Thirteen fates, thirteen lines, all threads intertwine..."

The fighting stopped, followed by a deafening silence.

"What's happening?" she called.

No answer.

Whatever it was, it succeeded in holding the crew transfixed, Etxarte included. Were the Harappans going to ram them? And here she sat, trapped below with no escape, like a dolphin doomed to drown in a fisherman's net.

Vividly did she recall her time as a prisoner on the Harappan galley—or rather, she remembered the terror she'd felt. The actual events returned to her memory only as blurry vignettes. Drowning was preferable to another experience like that, wasn't it?

A startling crash—off in the distance, thank the gods. More cheering. The crew began to sing.

Etxarte practically banged down the door. "The Romans sank the Harappan ship!" he exclaimed. "Come out and see."

"Finally!" She unbolted the door and hurried up top after him.

Sure enough, the sea boiled around the sinking enemy raider. As quickly as the storm had appeared, it dispersed.

"Leave it to the Romans to find a way to defeat our enemy!" exclaimed the captain.

The Roman sailors likewise cheered, hurling insults and curses at the dying beast they'd bested.

And there he stood, holding his head high in silent approval of his men's fine work.

Her heart leaped all the way up into her throat. She'd known it was his ship, the ship he named for her, the *Varina*. She couldn't say how, but she felt it the instant she saw her through the porthole, racing on the sea toward them.

They threw the trireme a line, and the Romans pulled the small mail ship to them so the tribune could have a word with the captain. As he stepped onto the deck, his eye fell on her.

She felt her heart might stop beating altogether. Once she gathered her wits, she flashed her prettiest smile. "You seem to be in the habit of rescuing me, tribune."

"*You* seem to be in the habit of getting yourself into trouble, my lady," he countered with a slight smirk of his own.

He looked so dashing and handsome in his battle armor, with his scarlet-crested helmet and cape flowing in the calming ocean breeze. Plowing the sea had tanned his olive skin and hardened his soldier's physique. To her, he looked like a hero from an epic poem, rolling in on a wave to her rescue.

Similar to nearly every other Roman she had met, he bore the same expression of pride and self confidence. Yet he was so unlike the other men of his country. Whenever he looked on her, it was always with admiration and respect, no condescension or delusions of his own superiority over her.

Marcus Duilius was a man who achieved great things on his own merits, without the need for standing on the shoulders of his people's accomplishments. Like his father, he was his own man, and didn't allow his plebeian origins to define the limits of his success. She adored him all the more for it.

The *barca* captain thanked Marcus for his assistance. "I thought surely our time had come." He removed his hat to wipe the nervous sweat beading through from his bald head.

Marcus snapped back to reality, and returned his attention to the captain. "Didn't Atlantis send an escort with you?"

"Their forces are stretched too thinly at the moment," Etxarte explained. "They had none to spare for a journey this far out."

"Interesting." He rubbed the dark stubble on his chin in thought. Gwenwhyfar thought it the dreamiest gesture in the world. "I haven't seen an Atlantean patrol vessel for at least a week. We must assume most of them have been destroyed or captured."

"Atlantean ships vulnerable!" the captain uttered. "I never dreamed of the day. This is terrible. How will I get my cargo to safety with those marauders at large along our shipping routes?"

"Allow me to escort you to Ker-Ys," Marcus offered.

Gwenwhyfar could not believe this turn of luck. She wanted to accept his offer, and forget about her mission altogether. *No. I can't throw aside my obligations, no matter how he confuses me.*

Etxarte spoke for her. "We're not going to Ker-Ys yet. We have another stop first."

"He's right," confirmed the captain. "I'm taking them first to the land of the Euskaldunak."

"The who?"

"You know them as the Vascones," Gwenwhyfar supplied. "I intend to make a treaty with them."

His face filled with admiration, which caused her knees to wobble. "A good idea. It would be my honor to escort you to the land of the Vascones, Lady Gwenwhyfar."

"Oh, there's no need to trouble yourself." she began lamely, locking her leg muscles.

"Not at all," he persisted. "I'm traveling in that direction anyway."

She tilted her head, puzzled. "You are?"

"My orders are to patrol the entrance to *Mare Nostram*."

"You mean the Middle Sea," Etxarte corrected.

The Roman returned a sarcastic squint. "That's what *you* call it. No enemy vessel is to pass the Pillars of Hercules. I'm to turn it back, or send it to the depths."

"We're a little far north from the Pillars, wouldn't you say?" the captain asked, still confused.

Marcus shifted from one foot to the other. "A Carthaginian captain sails in the vicinity with the same orders as mine. The uneasiness between our peoples makes it difficult to stay focused on our common enemy." He gripped the hilt of his sheathed sword. "I've extended my patrol route to avoid any...disagreements."

Gwenwhyfar remembered yet another reason she admired Marcus so. His tone suggested that he'd like nothing better than to give the other captain the fight he sought. Yet he chose instead to back down for the sake of the alliance. She knew full well that most Romans harbored far too much pride to take such a courageous first step.

"Your virtue is our fortune," she said. "We would be lost if you hadn't decided to sail this far north."

His lips turned upward at the compliment.

Etxarte crossed his arms. "Your services won't be necessary, tribune. We are grateful that you saved us, but we can manage from here on our own, *without* the assistance of Rome."

"Speak for yourself, Etxarte," the captain butted in. "On this vessel, I'm in charge. And if Tribune Duilius offers his assistance, then I intend to accept it."

"Good," said Marcus. "Ker-Ys is in dire need of these supplies, yes? In the interest of saving time, my lady, I can bring you to the Vascones via my ship, while your captain continues on to Ker-Ys."

His reasoning was sound. Even if she wanted to refuse—and she did not—civility dictated she must not. "Thank you."

Etxarte had no further arguments to present against the plan. No doubt he would think of more soon. He huffed below to gather up their travel bags.

Marcus chuckled after he disappeared. "He'll get over it."

Gwenwhyfar couldn't help her coloring cheeks as she placed her hand into his. His strong arm lifted her aboard the Varina.

IT SEEMED EVERY TIME he encountered the princess of Ker-Ys after a long absence, Marcus forgot how strikingly beautiful she was. This time proved no exception to the trend. It was all he could do not to freeze in mid stride when he saw her standing on the deck of the supply *barca*.

Her bewitching brown eyes, fringed with jet lashes never failed to pierce his very soul. Dressed in light green, she wore silver arm bands and a diadem to hold her dark ringlets out of her face. To him, she looked like an enchanting goddess from one of the epics she enjoyed reading.

Predictably, his powers of speech had dwindled in the moment as well. "You seem to be in the habit of getting yourself into trouble"?

What kind of response was *that*? He planted his knuckles between his eyes and groaned. She must view him as a complete dunderhead.

He could keep together his mental faculties around any woman—except her, the one woman he wanted to impress and woo more than anything. *Well, it's true*, he thought. *She is always getting herself into trouble.* But was that not the nature of women, to get into trouble?

All the gods in Hades! He wanted her anyway. For some reason unknown even to himself, he deemed her worth whatever trouble she put him through. Fate placed her within his reach yet again. This time, he would make the most of it.

Etxarte returned and boarded the *Varina* with two bags slung over his shoulder. As he passed, he mumbled in a voice meant for only Marcus' ears. "Don't even think about it."

Marcus pretended not to hear. The man had better not try to undermine his authority on his ship. Otherwise, disciplinary actions might be in order. He did not wish to take such drastic measures for Gwenwhyfar's sake, but if Etxarte tied his hands, then he would do what he must.

They bade the *Sea Harp* and her crew a safe voyage and turned northeast for the Bay of Biscane.

Etxarte should be aboard her, he wished, leaning on the railing as he watched them sail over the horizon.

Bad as Gwenwhyfar's guardian was, however, he wasn't nearly as disagreeable as her two brothers. Her entire family disapproved of him, come to think of it. But he intended to win them all over eventually. More than once, he considered carrying her off, and obtaining their permission after the fact. But Gwenwhyfar did not want that, he felt certain.

The subject of his thoughts appeared at his side. "Did you ever learn what happened to that band of Harappans fleeing Ker-Ys?" she asked.

He gave his full attention to his enchanting guest. "Yes, I defeated them myself. It happened just north of the bay we're headed for," he boasted. "They hid themselves in the forest a long time before attempting to escape to the sea on their makeshift rafts." He felt tempted to give her a full account of his military exploits since they last met, but then decided she may not hold much interest in hearing them all at once.

"I'm so glad you did," she said. "We worried all winter they might attack again. My mind can now rest at ease on that account."

"Happy to help." Immediately after he said it, he felt self conscious again. Couldn't he think of anything *halfway* intelligent to say?

Her smile grew warmer. "It's good to see you again, Marcus." Then just as quickly, the light faded from her eyes, and a dark cloud seemed to settle over her.

"What's wrong?" he asked.

She looked away toward the sea. "I'd rather not talk about it right now, if you don't mind."

"You're tired," he told her. "Ocean voyages tax the body, even for those of us accustomed to them. You should rest." He gestured below deck. "You can have my cabin. It isn't much, but it's the largest on the ship."

"That's gallant of you," she said with a coy bat of her lashes. "I wouldn't want to put you out, though."

"My lady, you've already done that," he joked, hoping to brighten her mood. "A princess deserves the best. I'm a Roman soldier. I can endure anything." He hoped the last bit didn't come across to her as bragging, even if it was true.

She thanked him, and went below.

He eyed her lovely form until she disappeared out of sight. Even fatigued, she had lost none of her loveliness. He turned back toward the setting sun and permitted a small smile to form on his face. Yes, he was a defeated man. What a sweet victory it must be for her, to have the vanquished so willingly surrender to her mercy.

He straightened his lips to a more neutral expression when he heard the sound of the centurion's footsteps behind him. Brutus gave him the evening report, after which Marcus informed him of the change in cabin assignments. His subordinate brought his fist to his chest, then went to carry out the orders.

Gwenwhyfar's status as royalty saved him from any embarrassing explanations to the crew about giving up his quarters for a woman, while he moved in temporarily with his first mate. Brutus, on the other hand, knew all about his feelings for Gwenwhyfar. He'd witnessed their parting on the dockway at Ker-Ys, when Marcus told her he would one day ask her to marry him.

The old salt had served his father, Gaius, in the war with Carthage. The admiral always credited his advice as leading him to victory at Mylae. When the Senate assigned Marcus his own flotilla, Gaius transferred his best officer to his son's command, to guide him as he had been guided. Marcus felt grateful for that.

He knew his centurion wouldn't question orders unless he saw it interfering with his ability to command. He'd even silence any hands he caught gossiping. *I must not give him any reasons to doubt my ability.* Real men—Roman men—did not lose their heads over Roman women, and especially not over a princess of barbarian Gaul.

As for Etxarte? Marcus chuckled to himself. *Dignitary or no, he can bunk with the crew. His warrior's pride will keep any complaints in check.*

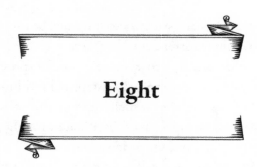

Eight

GWENWHYFAR STARED OUT to sea. Carrying through with her plan had just gotten that much more difficult. The Druids' prophecy turned over and over in her thoughts.

You must seek the seventh son of the seventh son. He is of your blood, the missing component that will complete your circle. Only with a complete circle will you find the means to stand against your foes.

A pod of gray whales glided on the surf off in the distance, blowing their glorious spray high into the air. They traversed the oceans with their families, surfacing for air many times each day, and re-submerging to continue their exploration of the mysterious fathoms below. She wondered if their lives were as simple as they appeared to her.

Footsteps from behind announced Marcus' approach. "We should arrive in three days, assuming the weather holds."

"Thank you," she responded, for a lack of anything better to say.

He glanced over at the whales. "A pity we must keep our distance. They can be dangerous, otherwise I'd move closer so you can observe them better."

"It is well. I've seen them closer before. They sometimes pass by Ker-Ys. But I appreciate the sentiment," she added sweetly.

She recalled one of her tutors telling her that a whale took but a single mate in its lifetime. If one of the two died, he'd said, the other would die soon afterward. *How fortunate I'm not a whale, then*, she thought. On the other hand, a whale had the freedom to choose her own mate. She didn't have her entire whale pod telling her who she may or may not marry. Or at least, Gwenwhyfar imagined it must be so.

Marcus stared at her. He shifted his weight from one foot to the other.

"You wish to say something?" she asked.

"Yes... I meant to say something." He looked down and examined the wooden railing. "But I forgot it when I looked at you. You're so beautiful. No woman has ever distracted me the way you do."

Considering his position and aims in life as a Roman, he must trust her a great deal to confide that to her. She surmised he might not admit that to most of his peers. It was exactly the way she felt about him.

"What were *you* thinking about?" he asked.

She turned back to face the sea. "Do you suppose whales' societies are anything like ours?"

He blinked. "I've never thought about them. They seem intelligent, as far as fishes come. Perhaps they are, though I doubt they're as complex as ours."

"That is my conclusion, too."

"Their day to day lives aren't any less difficult than ours," he continued, "if that's what you're wondering. I know little about whales, but I do know the sea. She's a treacherous, pitiless mistress, who often takes more than she gives. I wonder if even Neptune understands her fully."

He gently placed a roughened hand over hers. She felt the confidence in his touch. It filled her with yearning. More than anything, she wanted pour her heart out to him and let him fix all of her troubles. He would do it if she asked, even if it ruined them both. She withdrew her hand.

His eyes filled with hurt. "Why do you pull away? Two seasons ago, you said you loved me. I see that same ardor in your eyes now, yet something or someone has convinced you again that we can never be. You didn't believe that then. Why do you believe it now?"

"You can't understand," she said softly.

"Then *make* me understand," he grabbed her hand and placed it on his chest. He kept his voice low, lest any of the crew overhear them. "Feel how my heart beats for you, Gwenwhyfar. Make me understand!"

"You know my life is not my own. It never was. My fate was decided at my birth. Just like yours." No longer could she bear the intensity of his gaze. She looked away. Reminding him of his inferior social status made her feel like a shallow socialite. It felt petty, and she knew how acutely it wounded him coming from her.

"My fate *was* decided then," he conceded, a bitterness tinging his tone. "Most people never think beyond their birth. But if I had contented myself with everyone else's opinions of me, I wouldn't be the man I am today. People like us make our own destinies, Gwenwhyfar—and to the waves with the naysayers who oppose us."

He leaned toward her. "They allow the winds to decide how and what they think. We set our sails and make the wind work for us. They'll change their minds the instant we prove them wrong."

"If only it were that simple."

"It *is* that simple. I could spend all day listing reasons why we could never work." He took her by the shoulders and turned her to face him. "Instead I'll tell you one reason why we will: I love you. I'm committed to you. Is it because your guardian disapproves?"

Gwenwhyfar could not make herself look up. "That's only part of it."

"He will not withhold his blessing forever," he reasoned. "Etxarte loves you as I do. He wants you to find happiness. On that point he and I can agree. The rest will work itself out."

Desperately, she wanted to heed his words. His dogged determination couldn't help her people the way the Euskaldunak could. One day, Marcus might wield the power to help her in the way he wanted. But that day would come too late for Ker-Ys. If only she could afford to wait for him!

But she couldn't. If she did not do something now, her people might not survive the war.

"Speak to me," he implored. "Let us solve this problem together."

"I can't. I'm afraid you'll hate me when you know." She drew in trembling breaths to hold back her tears.

"How could I ever hate a wonderful, caring, accomplished woman like you? After all we have faced, I'm certain I can pass whatever test remains." He gently lifted her chin. The look in his adoring eyes brought tears to her own. "Even if our peoples were enemies, I would not hate you, Gwenwhyfar."

She bit her lip to keep it from quivering.

He released her, then set his jaw. "You love another man? Please, just tell me. I swear I won't get angry."

"No." She held her breath in order to hold back the sob that threatened to escape. "I don't love another man, Marcus."

His powerful shoulders relaxed. "That's all I need to know. As long as you love me, I will never abandon you."

Upon hearing his promise, there was no way should could tell him what she might need to do. "I want to be alone now." She made for the direction of her cabin.

He took her hand to stop her. "When you're ready to talk, you need only send for me. I will listen to whatever you must say. Please don't shut me out for long."

She nodded, but again couldn't bear to look at his face. With great reluctance, he released her hand.

When she reached her cabin, she curled up into her hammock for a cry. "Oh, why did he have to be so wonderful?"

MARCUS TOOK HIS USUAL place on the uppermost deck of the *Varina*.

What had gone wrong? Time had a way of changing things, an undisputed fact. But had so much time passed?

Gwenwhyfar loved him still, of that he felt certain. At first, he believed she'd fallen back into the trap of trying to please Etxarte and her brothers. Now, he saw the issue went deeper than that, something she felt afraid to tell him.

Whatever it was, he wouldn't like it. Was she afraid he might lash out at her once he knew? He must convince her to open up to him. They would face the trial together. He'd come too far already to fail a simple test of his love.

To pass the time, he slipped into the familiar routine of command: the officers' reports, the calculating of their speed and distance covered, the swells rising and falling beneath his feet. *A yare ship, my* Varina. *If only I knew how to handle a woman of flesh and blood as well as my lady of wood.*

Yes, he understood the sea about as well as a mortal man could. The struggle for life in the ocean realm was no less difficult than on land, though it felt far simpler —not unlike the lot of that pod of whales shrinking into the distance. He silently bade them a good journey, and went to make his rounds.

When he reached the middle deck, he saw Etxarte marching toward him with the clear intent of a serious discussion. He resisted the urge to retreat back up to the command deck.

"How long will you persist in tormenting her?" he demanded.

"I don't know what you mean, captain," Marcus feigned. Useless though it was to ignore him, he continued with his inspections with complete mastery of his features.

"She's already suffered enough at the hands of your people."

That cracked him, though he kept his tone calm. "What bothers you more, Etxarte? That I'm not of your people, or that I am of the *Roman* people, hmm?"

Etxarte's mouth hardened. "Both."

At least the Breizhian had the sense to keep his voice down, though Marcus felt certain the crew would drink in most of this conversation anyway. Keeping a secret on a ship was nigh impossible.

"Your futures lie at the ends of different paths," the man continued. "You must stop pursuing her."

Marcus examined the knots of ropes holding the sails. "The only way that will happen is if she tells me that herself."

"How can she, when you won't let her?"

Now Marcus' control slipped altogether. "I don't get the impression she wants me to. What I *do* see is that few people want to consider her happiness. You all want her to play her part in *your* plans. You won't give her the option of making her own way."

"The needs of Ker-Ys must come first."

"What makes you think she doesn't factor that into her plans, just because she may not see the same vision for Ker-Ys that you do?"

Condemnation glowed Etxarte's eyes. "And I naturally you see yourself and Rome in that vision."

Marcus glared back. "If she wishes it, yes."

"Has she said she would marry you? I mean since the last time you saw her?"

"She said she would think about it," he returned, feeling less confident. Etxarte folded his arms in triumph.

"So she said no."

"'I will think about it,'" he countered, "is not the same thing as 'no.'"

"Close enough. Don't fall for someone who isn't willing to catch you, Roman," he warned. "Ker-Ys will not become some dependency that pays tribute to you."

Satisfied at winning the debate, the Breizhian left. To go talk Gwenwhyfar into seeing things his way, no doubt.

Marcus let him go and finished his inspections. Doubts filled his mind. Did she believe he intended to bring Ker-Ys under the dominion of Rome? He forced himself to acknowledge that at one time, that was exactly what he wished. He, too, had once been guilty of seeing her as a mere component of his own plans. *No wonder she hesitates to confide in me.*

Giving up his own ambitions was not easy. He would have to choose what he deemed more important to him. Up to then, he'd imagined he could do mighty deeds for Rome and marry Gwenwhyfar. He'd already promised to resign from his career after the war was over.

Maybe that isn't enough? Maybe she needs me much sooner than that?

Were Gaia there, she would remind him that there was more to the world than the realms of Rome, glorious and beloved though their homeland was to her. His little sister spoke her opinions too freely.

She was right, of course. As Gwenwhyfar's consort, he'd have opportunities for power in Ker-Ys that would take generations to build in Roman society. Unless he wanted to build up his own army and conquer his own people.

No, he did not desire that.

Returning to the command deck, he stared out over the horizon, as though it might somehow reveal his future to him.

Not surprisingly, all he saw was an endless stretch of water.

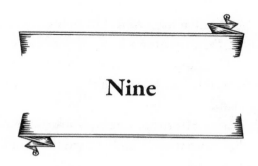

Nine

KENDA HAD NOT EATEN with his bare fingers in forever. He *loved* it. All those civilized years using Atlantean eating utensils melted away. He felt again like a young man in Nubia, when he lived in wedded bliss with his beloved Jamilia.

Glancing over at his companion, he watched Shahin scoop his stew of plantains and rice into a sticky ball, then insert it into his mouth. The Persian adapted like a pro. Kenda remembered that his partner traveled far more extensively than even he.

To tell the truth, *anything* tasted better than the slop that kept them alive those many weeks at sea. They would have to eat it on the return voyage. Kenda focused his attention on the delicious meal in front of him.

King Ashoka proved a generous and attentive host. They had not met him as of yet, yet Kenda already inclined to form a favorable opinion of him, since his majesty had seen to their needs while they waited for an audience.

Outside the dining courtyard, workers labored to erect a glorious monument. Apparently, King Ashoka had converted to some new philosophy. As a result, he put aside his former violent ways to embrace the ideals of a dead sage referred to as "the Enlightened One." His bones had been recently uncovered on that spot, and Ashoka demonstrated his devotion by building a massive tomb for the remains of the Buddha.

Kenda shrugged, and took another bite of his chicken. *All the better for us*, he thought. Far easier for a lover of peace to come around to their plight than a bloodthirsty tyrant. Still, he felt uneasy, and it wasn't only because of their mission. Nor was it the anxiety a person felt when visiting a foreign land.

Shahin felt it, too. His nervousness seemed to increase the closer they came to India. Once more, Kenda sensed the man hid something. Whatever his secret, it was big.

SEVERAL HOURS LATER, Kenda and Shahin wandered through the walled garden adjacent to the dining area. A large, ornate fountain trickled in the center, its echo breaking up the sound of their voices. Eavesdropping on their conversation without detection would prove impossible for anyone who dared try it. The palace architect must have designed that way.

"The trouble with being punctual is that nobody's there to appreciate it," Kenda observed, growing impatient.

"Careful of snakes," the Persian warned him. "The deadliest in the world inhabit these lands. Mind the tiny ones." He'd told Kenda everything he needed to know about India in little nuggets like that since the day they sailed out of Atlantis harbor.

"I'll remember that," he replied. He'd seen his share of snakes in his own homeland of Nubia, from the hooded cobra to the common asp.

He noted Shahin's warning, and continued to view the exotic flowers. Shahin grasped his wrist to stop him from picking one of the flowers. Lifting a large leaf of the plant, he revealed a small brown snake taking shelter from the afternoon heat—right underneath the flower. Had he not uncovered the creature, Kenda might have put his hand just close enough.

"One bite from this fellow," said Shahin, "and you'll not live to taste the delights of the evening feast."

Kenda felt his blood run cold. Such a small snake seemed insignificant and harmless to a mighty warrior. If it bit him, he would have dismissed it as no worse than a mosquito. "Thanks for the warning," he said.

He'd better remember to check his bed linens that night. With a man as shady as Shahin, one never knew. The chamberlain appeared from a nearby archway.

"The Mighty King Ashoka will see you now," he announced

"Well," Shahin remarked with his usual carefree facade, "that certainly is timely. Dare we hope we're one of the king's more interesting visitors today?"

"I'm not sure if I want that," Kenda said through the side of his mouth.

"Believe me," countered Shahin, the volume of his voice dropping, "you want it."

They followed the doorkeeper through a maze of breezeways, each ornate and breathtaking in its own right. Kenda found himself wishing to spend at least a few minutes examining the intricate artwork. But their guide hurried along. The whirlwind of color and patterns crescendoed in a massive throne room.

Ashoka sat in the center, surrounded by his advisors. The king poured over a scroll, while slaves fanned him. He sat proud upon his throne, thoughtfully twirling the edge of his dark mustache. His clothes of fine silk, together with the sizable diamond affixed in his turban, attested to his wealth and scale of his trading empire.

He's younger than I expected, Kenda thought. In truth, he was close to his own age, but somehow, he had imagined a much older man. He searched Shahin to see if he, too, held different expectations. But as usual, the Persian's expression remained neutral.

"Ambassador Kenda Ptah and his assistant, representing the Democracy of Atlantis," announced the doorkeeper.

Ashoka seemed not to hear the introduction, and continued to ponder his reading material. Shahin did not need to remind his companion to wait for the sovereign to address them before speaking.

After several minutes passed, Ashoka still did not look up from his scroll. Just as a weary yawn threatened to escape from Kenda's mouth, the king looked up—or rather, he looked down at his visitors, for his dais stood above the rest of the chamber. "Representatives of Atlantis," he greeted.

Kenda bowed low. "Your majesty." Like most Atlanteans, he held the idea of kings with little esteem, because of their propensity for tyranny. But he respected the customs of others in view of his position as a diplomat.

Ashoka's face was stern, though his voice calm. "So Atlantis has deigned to pay Us a visit at last? To what do We owe this honor?"

"Our visit is shamefully overdue, Majesty," Kenda conceded. "We come seeking your council. But may I add that I personally am pleased it has come to this, since I am the one who enjoys the privilege of experiencing the magnificence of your kingdom and of your presence?"

"You may," the king permitted. "But you have not answered my question." He knew the purpose of their visit, yet formalities must be observed.

"Majesty," Kenda commenced, "several lands in the West have been attacked by a people unknown to us. We believe they originated in or near your own great kingdom."

Ashoka's mustache turned up at the corners along with his lips. "Are We to understand that Atlantis feels threatened by these people?" He picked a piece of fruit from a nearby dish. "We were under the impression that such a scenario is unthinkable, and only the subject of playwrights and philosophers' hypotheses."

Curse that meddling Plato and his stylus! "It is true," he admitted. Werta may not like it, but Kenda decided it best to err on the side of the truth. Ashoka would take anything else as an insult. To a king as wise as he, it would have been.

"These people are unlike any other Atlantis has encountered before," Kenda explained. "They fear no pain, nor hunger, nor weariness. They did not attack us directly, but we believe it is only a matter of time before they do. Nothing can stop them."

"Atlantis cannot defeat them?" marveled the king.

"We have kept them at bay. We defeated them only once, at a small city in northern Gaul, and that was a pyrrhic victory. The more we kill, the more rise up to take their places. Soon, every land in the West will have spent its manpower and resources trying to keep them at bay."

Ashoka raised a brow, and looked straight at Kenda. "Including Atlantis?"

"Yes," he said, not daring to lie to such a leader.

"Hmmm..." The king stroked the arm of his throne of carved ivory, the tone of his voice changing. "In exchange for your humility in acknowledging that, Ambassador Ptah, I will give you the information you seek." It was the first time he used the pronoun *I* instead of the royal *We*.

"Harappa was a great civilization that ruled this land and far beyond, long ago. The wisest say they angered the gods with their pride. Only Kali, the goddess of death, indulged them in their sin. But she could not protect them from the ire of the other deities.

"They were defeated and their great city destroyed, though their descendants survived the ages. We believed the Greek conqueror destroyed the last of them— until I faced them myself. That was when I realized I was not any different."

He rose from his throne to pace, regret dogging his steps. "In building my Empire, I stopped at nothing. No amount of pleading from the innocent could stay the hand of my ambition of conquest. To my deepest regret, their blood has stained my soul, and my guilt haunts me to this day. Only the teachings of the Enlightened One have succeeded in granting me peace."

Kenda recalled the grand monument he observed from the courtyard. It would stand as a testament to Ashoka's gratitude long after he passed from this mortal plain.

Ashoka continued. "I first encountered them as a newly-crowned king. In those days, I stopped at nothing to get what I wanted, no matter how many people suffered or died. Alexander inspired my quest. If a westerner could accomplish such feats, why not I?" He paused, as though expecting an answer.

Kenda held his hands behind his back and stared at the patterns of the mosaic floor. He had no diplomatic answer to give to a king.

"A fair question," Shahin filled in.

Kenda dipped his head in agreement.

His justification satisfied the ruler. "Into the valley of the Indus I went. That's where I met them. Ironic that I would face the descendants of those who rose up against Alexander. He did not defeat them, but I vowed to succeed where the Greek failed.

"In the end, my success in this regard was like my counterpart. I did not win against them, but neither did they overpower me. One day, they simply vanished, retreating to the Western Wilderness or the sea. Before they left, their high priestess paid me a visit. Lavanya warned me they would return again to take my kingdom from me, along with the rest of the world."

Shahin straightened. The reaction was so subtle that Kenda might have missed it, had he not turned to his aide to guess his opinion. *Interesting*, he thought, making a note to inquire about it later. "Can his majesty tell us where they learned their advanced warfare?"

"Their pact with Kali grants them control over the natural realm. They use this power with the intention of establishing a new kingdom for Kali's children."

"Kali's children are few in number," Kenda pointed out.

The king's face turned grave. "Yes. They believe every other human being must die to slake her lust for blood, for Kali commands them to purge the world of unbelievers."

Kenda knew this, of course, from his own experience. Yet hearing it spoken aloud by a foreign ruler drove the point home with a fresh wave of urgency. "That is why we must stop them, your majesty," he reiterated. "Because they will not stop until they've carried out their evil purpose, even if it means destroying themselves in the process."

"Only displeasing Kali gives them cause for unease," Ashoka concurred, "for she was the only deity who did not forsake them."

Kenda steepled his hands together to convey the authority of his opinion. "A struggle the likes of which the world has never seen is about to ensue. Atlantis believes the only way to stand against this foe is for us to band together."

Ashoka sat back down. "Atlantis must also realize that is much easier said than done. Some will see the necessity right away. Only great catastrophe will wake up others. Will we all come together in time?" He paused to consider his own question.

Shahin spoke up. "'The journey of a thousand miles begins with one step,' your majesty."

"Indeed, it does." He clapped his hands, and a servant appeared with a fan for walking. "Come. We will consult the wise monks."

They followed him out through the courtyard to another breezeway leading outside of the palace. Elaborate archways held up the roof, though no railings stood between them and the bustling streets below. Both the palace behind and the building ahead boasted of few windows and no other entrances. Clearly, only the inhabitants of either dwelling were permitted to interact with each other.

Kenda glanced behind at Shahin, who strode behind in the dead center of the walkway. His face paled, though he kept his eyes facing forward, allowing none of the sights, sounds, or smells below to deviate him from the entrance to the other building. *Afraid of heights, are we?*

Facing forward with no small amusement, Kenda filed that little nugget of gold away for future blackmail. Were they not a part of Ashoka's dignified entourage, he might have thrown his head back and laughed hard at the discovery.

As they neared the other side, a loud buzzing sound met them. It felt like the entrance to a beehive. Perhaps he'd laughed too soon at Shahin's apprehension? Did he, as usual, know something Kenda did not?

Sometime after entering through a set of large, red doors, he realized the sound was not from bees, but of many human voices. Chanting drifted up to the domed ceiling. The smell of incense told him they now entered a temple.

A man in red robes and a shaved head appeared and bowed to the king. Without a word, he turned to strike a gong in the corner. A few minutes passed, and another monk appeared.

"Mighty king," he greeted with his hands pressed together.

The king returned the gesture. "Wise one, I come seeking your counsel."

The monk's hands parted. "What quandary troubles his majesty?"

"The Cult of Kali, and their connection to Harappa."

The monk's face remained neutral, though Kenda detected the slightest twinge of nervousness in his hands at the mention of their foe. Had this kingdom suffered more recent encounters than Ashoka let on?

"Let us consult the sacred scrolls," he said quietly. "If his majesty will follow me."

They left the vestibule of the temple and entered a garden. Its design was simplistic, yet thought provoking. On the other side of the garden stood doors leading to a library. Their guide pushed them open without knocking.

Inside, monks sat on their knees all around, reading or writing graceful calligraphy with paintbrushes. Even from inside this quiet room, the buzzing sound of chant could be heard coming from other parts of the monastery.

Ashoka took a seat in the room's only chair. Kenda supposed the monks kept it there for that exact purpose.

Realizing the ignorance of their guests regarding protocol, the monk turned to them at whispered in Greek, "You are free to browse our collection."

Shahin placed his hands together and bowed his head. "We are honored, wise one."

Kenda followed his example.

After the monk went off to search for the information, Shahin explained. "They've bestowed a great honor on us. They don't usually grant this privilege to outsiders."

"Delightful," he whispered back. "I suggest we take them up on the offer so as not to insult them."

The Persian's lips curved into a wry crescent. "You're learning faster than I thought you would."

As they were in full view of everyone, he bit down his retort. Besides, he possessed a delicious bite of blackmail about Shahin to chew on, one that would keep him satisfied for a while.

They browsed for some time. Wherever the particular scroll was, the monks must have to dig deep into their archives to find it. Ashoka meanwhile dozed while his servant fanned away the afternoon heat.

Right away, Kenda discovered he could not read most of the scrolls contained in the library. "Can you read this gibberish?" he asked Shahin.

"Some of them. But most of them are in an ancient form of Sanskrit, of a particular dialect I never studied. The Persian scrolls are texts I have already read many times since childhood."

"We must have perused these shelves an hour, and I've seen only one Greek book —one!"

Shahin rendered a sympathetic shrug, but had nothing more to offer.

At long last, the monk reappeared. "It is here," he announced.

Ashoka snorted, and opened his eyes. "Yes?"

The monk unrolled his scroll. "A prophesy from one of the Enlightened Ones." He read the poem aloud in its original language.

Shahin whispered the translation to Kenda as best as he could understand. "The children of Kali...seek to destroy the world...bathe the world in a rebirth of blood...the peoples of all lands must band together...a great mountain, or perhaps an island, sinks to the depths of the sea." He squinted. "I'm sorry, that's the best I can offer."

"It's good enough," Kenda grumbled. Was every philosopher on earth intent upon Atlantis' demise?

True, his adopted people had made their share of enemies down through the ages. But not of the entire world, and certainly not of any Indian kingdom before the Harappans showed up on the scene.

"That is all the Enlightened One wrote on the matter," said the monk. "Does his majesty require anything else?"

"No, thank you, wise one. May the wisdom of the Buddha smile down upon you." He folded his hands and made for the exit.

Kenda followed the king with a surreal awareness of the sights around him, his reveling in Shahin's insecurities forgotten.

The prophesy bore an eerie similarity to the poem that slip of a princess discovered, when he stumbled into that secret passage under the great library in Atlantis with her. A hypothesis formed in his mind. Common knowledge dictated that the Atlantean librarians had gathered various books and knowledge from all over the world. Had they long ago succeeded in piecing together these similar prophecies?

The Followers of Erykanis, the oracle at Delphi, the Druids, the Buddhist monks, and who could say how many others; they all pointed to the destruction of Atlantis. Had the librarians known all along?

Few people were chosen to serve at the library. Those fortunate souls were often the relatives and children of the elder librarians. He remembered the defensive manner the librarian displayed in ordering he and Gwenwhyfar to leave. At the time, he dismissed his suspicions, chalking it up to Werta's timely summons. *Timely indeed!*

Up to this point, he found himself so caught up in the mission that he had not thought much about the event. But now it all came together: the librarians *did* know, and they were hiding it from the Atlantean people. Might they be in cahoots with the Followers of Erykanis? Who else knew about this?

"I am tired, and have much to think upon," said Ashoka, when they returned to the throne room. "Rest in your chambers until I summon you."

Kenda uttered some automatic response, then left.

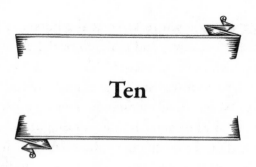

Ten

"NEVER AGAIN DID I THINK to set eyes upon the land of my mother." Etxarte's venerable face shined with pride.

His comment caught the interest of Centurion Brutus. "You are Vascone?"

"Many in Ker-Ys are," he informed the other veteran. "My parents sided with Gwenwhyfar's grandfather during the feud. My father saw a greatness to Erwan that he felt our own tribe lacked."

While they spoke, Marcus scanned the coastline before them. A small Euskaldunak fishing village stood on the beach. Though the sea lied to the west of the settlement, all the houses faced east, toward the rising sun. The land seemed harsh and barren, a rough country where only the strongest survived. No wonder Carthage never tried to conquer them. Why fight over undesirable territory? He certainly did not deem it worth the cost of a campaign.

In the scrub covered hills above, echoing shouts reverberating from all around the cliffs to the sea below. More calls followed them. Marcus and his men instinctively drew their swords.

"They're letting each other know we're here," Gwenwhyfar explained. The sadness in her voice increased the closer they came to the Vascone shores.

He wished she would confide in him again, as she had those times when they spoke together in Atlantis. What had he done to give her cause to mistrust him? He could use some of that whispering arch ambiance right about now.

Determined to continue the conversation, he asked, "What is he like, this Enri Loiol?"

"We've never met," she explained. "Our grandfathers were brothers. Etxarte hasn't seen him, either. But he is the seventh son of a seventh son. That is why the Druids say he holds the key to my people's survival."

"What happened to his six elder brothers?" Marcus asked, tilting his head in suspicion. "I imagine some were killed fighting your people in the war with Carthage. But not all of them are dead. Tradition dictates Enri was born to be their leader. To challenge that fact would be to question the will of the gods."

Etxarte joined them. "If he's like the rest of the Euskaldunak, he's a stout fellow, with long ears." He waved his hands around his own ears to demonstrate.

Gwenwhyfar chuckled.

Now that Marcus looked for it, he saw the Etxarte's ears were also rather long. "What exactly caused this dispute?" he asked.

Etxarte shook his head. "It's too complicated for an outsider to understand."

"Too complicated for *me* to understand," said Gwenwhyfar. "Even if the official reason has been explained countless times."

"You'd better show more interest than that if you want this to work," Etxarte warned her. "Otherwise, he won't listen to you. Believe me, I know my people."

He *will* listen to her, Marcus vowed. He faced his centurion. "Send out the landing boats, and inform them of our intentions." Then he turned to Etxarte. "I assume they speak Greek?"

He crossed his arms over his chest. "My people aren't ignorant, tribune."

Marcus lifted his shoulder in a half shrug. "I'm prepared for anything. Why don't you go with Brutus to make sure?"

Etxarte huffed, though he followed the centurion into the landing boat anyway.

THE SUN SANK LOW ON the horizon when Brutus and Etxarte returned. "They've agreed to meet with us, tribune," the centurion reported with obvious reservations, "on the condition that we allow them to blindfold us there and back. Their leader promises us safe passage until we return to our ship. Personally, sir, I wouldn't—"

Marcus held up a hand for silence. "Thank you, centurion." He looked to Gwenwhyfar. "Please don't take this the wrong way, but I must ask if you believe we can trust them?"

She nodded. "You are wise to be cautious. I can tell you that if a promise has been given, you may depend upon it."

"That's a relief." He trusted her judgment, though his would not trust the Vascones before they proved themselves to him.

"You don't have to come with us, Marcus," she said, running the edge of a sleeve between her fingers. "You've already done enough by bringing us here. More than anyone else would have."

He could tell that she felt as uneasy as he did about the whole venture. "I won't abandon you."

Etxarte snorted, but said nothing.

"Thank you," she said, still fiddling with the fold of her sleeve.

Marcus got the distinct impression she felt torn over whether or not she wanted him to go along. Whatever awaited her in regards to her cousin, she was afraid of him seeing it. Exactly what kind of people were these Vascones that their own cousin must fear them?

"What sort of demeanor did the messenger project?" he asked his officer.

"Well, sir," said Brutus, "I know it's an overused expression to say he smiled with his eyes but, he did smile with his eyes. It was the smile of a predator. He would have liked to kill me where I stood. And I think he might have, if Etxarte wasn't with me."

"Charming people," Marcus remarked. "Anything else?"

"Only that I don't recommend trusting them, sir. But you already know that."

Marcus exhaled. "I appreciate your honesty. Return to shore with Etxarte. Tell them we agree to the terms and will meet them on the beach in the morning. That will be all."

Brutus brought his fist to his chest, though he did not agree with the command.

Marcus didn't blame him. Without Gwenwhyfar's opinion, he would not have trusted the word of the Vascones, either.

The princess had stood in silence for the entire exchange. "I need to rest before tomorrow," she said, heading below for her cabin. Again, she seemed near tears.

For the sake of his men, he kept to formalities. "Is there anything I can get you, my lady?"

Distress broke through her cool demeanor. "Thank you, tribune, no." She disappeared below deck.

"Eh, women," mumbled the centurion as they climbed back into the boat. "Haven't met one yet half as reliable as a good horse."

"Among my people, a woman holds a great deal of value," Etxarte countered. "But I agree, a good horse is like a member of the family."

Marcus refrained from shooting a hostile look at them. Etxarte and Brutus already knew of his amour, it was true. But he saw no need to demonstrate to either of them just how far he'd fallen.

WHEN THE LANDING PARTY returned for the night, Brutus went below to check on the rowers.

Meanwhile, Marcus watched Etxarte sit down among the deck hands and busy himself by tying knots. A theory entered his mind, the implications of which sent his emotions reeling. High time he got to the bottom of this matter. Etxarte knew the reasons for Gwenwhyfar's distress, and he suspected it would not take much to goad the captain into revealing what he needed to know.

With a gesture, he sent his sailors off to busy themselves with other tasks.

Etxarte looked up. "What do you want?"

"Tell me," he said, fingering a strand of rope in need of repair, "what is so distressing about a treaty?"

His eyes dropped to the rope in his hands. "Nothing, tribune. Absolutely nothing. Words on paper."

"Then why does your charge find herself in tears over mere words on paper?"

The elder man frowned. "You know how emotional women are."

"Stop giving me the runaround, Etxarte," he demanded. "I want answers!"

"Words on paper," Etxarte repeated with a snort. "They mean nothing. Blood ties are the only thing that truly bind. The Euskaldunak understand this. And so does Gwenwhyfar."

His words fell on Marcus like a broken column of marble.

Blood ties. How had he been such a fool as not to see it before? To his horror, the threads all came together in his mind. In order to form the alliance, Gwenwhyfar intended to marry the Vascone leader, Enri Loiol.

"They were betrothed at birth," Etxarte continued. "But after Lord Erwan's death, Tierney decided to ally with Rome instead. Against my advice." He rose, then went below deck. Pausing at the top of the ladder, he added, "You should have listened to my warning, boy. Now you have hurt both yourself and her."

Marcus felt his entire body go numb.

Mercifully, Brutus returned a few minutes later. "If I may say sir, you have a difficult day ahead of you. You don't need to take a watch tonight. We can handle it."

He returned a noncommittal reply and made for his cabin. Once there, he drove his fist into the hull. The blow didn't make a dent in the hard wood. Gritting his teeth, he leaned against the wall, allowing the pain throb all the way up to his shoulder.

He should never have come here. But what else could he have done? A younger version of him might have sent her on her way and sailed off without a single glance over his shoulder. "Woman of Gaul, what have you done to me?" he uttered, barely finding his breath.

There he had stood, pouring his heart out to her, and all the while she'd tried to tell him she was on her way to marry another man. He would not have listened even if she did him, he realized. Of course she couldn't bring herself to tell him the entire truth!

Surely, there were other possible allies to help her? Yes, there were—but no matter which one she chose, the outcome remained the same. She must marry into their tribe to forge an alliance. Such was the way of the Breizhians, her people. Their old dealings with the Atlanteans had sown a mistrust for words written on papyrus.

Because of a primitive superstition, Marcus would lose the woman he loved.

Not for the first time, he cursed his own lowly birth. If only he were a patrician, like Petronius, then he could offer to marry her himself, and Ker-Ys could join with Rome once again. Or, if he'd won more battles and gained glory sooner in this war, his plebeian origins might not pose an obstacle. But the way things currently stood, he hadn't yet earned the privilege of representing his people in a marriage alliance. Nothing he could do would change the way this insane world operated. He hated it—the world, the Harappans, Rome, Ker-Ys.

Most of all, he hated himself for being an impotent weakling, unable to reshape his destiny the way he'd so confidently believed up to that moment. His fist throbbed with sharp pain. For a few seconds, he wondered if he'd broken his hand. Did it matter? What was the use of anything? What a sentimental milksop he'd become, letting his life's ambition go to pieces—over a woman!

He took several deep breaths. "Harden your heart, Roman," he rasped.

Plebeian or patrician, a Roman was a Roman. Like his people, he greatness remained part of his destiny. Though his entire being desired Gwenwhyfar to have a part of his glorious future, he forced himself to admit she wasn't a requirement for its fulfillment.

A knock wounded at the door. "Sir?"

"What is it, centurion?" he growled.

"I heard a loud noise, sir. I thought...I didn't know what to think."

"It's nothing," he said. "Wait." He opened the door, holding his injured hand behind his back. "I forgot to give you tomorrow's orders. Once we're ashore in the morning, I want you to make another run past the Pillars, then return here."

Brutus' face turned a beat red, the hue visible even in the dim lighting. "Tribune! That will take at least a week!"

Marcus ignored his protests. "When you return, wait a day here for me. If I'm not on shore, make another sweep, and return again. If I don't come the second time, you must assume I'm missing in action and continue the patrol until you receive new orders."

"But, tribune—"

"Is that clear?" he interrupted.

The gray-haired centurion struggled to gain his control.

Marcus appreciated Brutus' devotion. He also appreciated the difficulty he must have had in accepting orders from a superior much younger than himself.

At last, he brought his fist to his chest. "Yes, tribune."

"That is all." He closed the door.

He asked a good deal with such strange orders, and after going so far off their original course. Yet he knew that Brutus would never fail in his duty to his commanding officer.

Duty. Honor. Loyalty to one's people. Those were things he, Brutus, and Gwenwhyfar understood well. For a leader, personal desires must always come second to the greater good. They'd all been raised on those values.

His Gwenwhyfar was a strong, determined woman, who would never fail to lead her people. A quality—one of many—which made him love her so much. And that was the reason he would not fail her.

He promised to see her safely to this Vascone, Loiol. That was exactly what he intended to do. Should the situation call for it, he would stand with his head high and watch her wed the Euskaldunak man. Afterwards, he would continue alone on his path of destiny as a great hero of Rome.

From the deepest depths of his heart, he hoped the situation would not call for it.

GWENWHYFAR TRIED TO stop the tears from flowing from her eyes. Once she left the deck she could no longer hold them back. *Better to release them now instead of later in front of Enri*, she thought.

She must tell Marcus the truth before then. He deserved to know the risks after all he had done for her.

But how could she tell him? It would break his heart! The crestfallen look on his face would kill her, she felt sure of it. But if she did, how could she hold to her course? How could she tell him that, no matter how much she loved him, she might have to marry another man? She did not wish to marry Enri, but she did not hold the power to guarantee that necessity would not demand that of her.

She sank to the floor, quietly sobbing in defeat. It was hopeless.

A loud thump sounded from Marcus' cabin next door, jarring her from her melancholy. Her breath caught in her throat. Gods help her, he *knew*.

Either he deduced his own conclusions, or had wormed it out of Etxarte. But whichever the case, he hadn't learned it from her. He must think her a coward. She hated herself for that.

Panic seized her. *I can't do this!*

All around her, the sounds of the ship turned surreal. Her mind numbed together with her body. She doubted she'd sleep that night.

THE NEXT MORNING, THE landing party stood ready on deck. At Brutus' insistence, handful of the marines stood ready to accompany them ashore. Marcus acknowledged it was a good precaution.

Marcus put on his best tunic and armor on board. Tying his belt, he shoved the hilt of the hanging sword into his injured hand. It had ached the entire night. Not that he could have slept even without an injury. No time remained for the ship surgeon to take a look at it, however. He must wait until Brutus returned.

With a determined stride, he opened the door and made his way to the upper deck.

ETXARTE KNOCKED ON Gwenwhyfar's door. "It's time."

She composed herself, then followed him to the ladder. A sick, twisting pain formed in her stomach. How could she face Marcus?

Etxarte put a reassuring hand on her back. "You're doing the right thing."

Without a reply, she stepped on deck with her head held high.

Marcus waited, arrayed in his formal armor, its polished surface shining in the daylight despite passing clouds. He gestured toward the waiting boat, "My lady."

She lowered herself down and sat in the front to avoid seeing the hurt on his face.

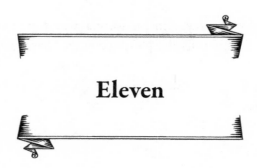

Eleven

THE WAY TO THE STRONGHOLD of the Vascones wound up a steep and rocky path. Their steps might have been easier, if they didn't have blindfolds tied across their eyes.

Marcus hoped their guides treated Gwenwhyfar better than they were treating him. He tried to listen for clues concerning her, but heard only the scraping of their party's footsteps across the rising path.

His guide scolded him in his strange language, then yanked his arm to one side. Marcus didn't need to understand the actual words to perceive that he'd nearly stepped over the edge of the cliff side. He returned a grunt of thanks.

They were heading into the mountains, that much he knew. He guessed they would go that way earlier when he'd studied the drab, misty peeks rising above the sea from his ship. That same mist now chilled his bare arms and legs. Spring had arrived late in this land, as it had everywhere else. He tightened his muscles to keep from shivering.

Marcus refused to adopt the effeminate custom of wearing *braccae* to cover his legs like these Vascones. He never intended to mention this view to Gwenwhyfar, since the men of her people likewise wore the wool leggings. But if Etxarte or her brothers ever pushed him, he might let his opinion slip. That, after all, was why Rome would conquer the world, because her men were strong and could endure any elements Mother Earth sent their way.

At least an hour passed before he felt a flat surface under his sandals. Words exchanged, and they entered the settlement. The chatter of people surrounded them. Their language sounded similar to the Atlantean tongue, but even he recognized significant differences.

They continued on through the fortress, passing through six gates up a steep and uneven path of rocks.

THE SOUND OF RUSHING water echoed off the high stone walls. Gwenwhyfar could not tell where the river lied. It sounded like it rushed passed them just on the other side of the wall to her right, though she surmised the sound was but an echo from far below in the valley.

Chilly, damp air penetrated to her bones—not unlike the cold she often felt at sea. Daybreak came later in the mountains than at sea or in flatter areas, she knew well, and she hoped the sun wouldn't take much longer to rise high enough to warm her chilled limbs.

Behind her, Marcus followed without the slightest sound of difficulty or complaint. She couldn't imagine venturing out in this land without the wool leggings beneath her tunic and boots to keep her feet warm and protected from the sharp crags.

Her heart warmed in admiration of his manly strength. *He's both strong and intelligent, like Ulysses*, she thought. *Far more worthy than Enri can ever be—or any other man for that matter. I cannot doubt his devotion to me.* With Marcus, she would have a partner in marriage, not some tyrant who saw her only as a mill for churning out his heirs.

Then she remembered the folly of loving him. No matter his virtues or the intensity of her feelings for him, the needs of Ker-Ys must come first. Enri was the one who held the power to save her people, not Marcus.

I make my own destiny, she'd heard the rising plebeian say once. Why could she not do the same? Why couldn't she, too, captain the voyage of her own life?

They heard what sounded like the lifting of a large metal object. A portcullis? she wondered. A dog barked, and soon she felt the presence of a crowd of people surrounding them.

Etxarte constantly told her during lessons that she could accomplish whatever she set her mind to; yet even he seemed believe this was her only course. He likely held out some hope that once she met Enri, she might fall in love with him, by the sheer quality that he led the proud Euskaldunak.

Why can't he understand I want Marcus! I've never loved any other man, and I'm certain I never will.

The guides removed their blindfolds.

They stood in a large courtyard of stone. The gathered people watched them pass with unabashed curiosity, their rough faces peering through their weathered clothing. She did not blame them. The Princess of the Breizhians, one of their own warriors who'd lived in exile for over a generation, and a Roman tribune with his marines—an odd fellowship if ever there was one.

Yet even from their isolated stronghold, they must know that the world had undergone drastic changes of late?

Strange times, indeed. The wheels of her thoughts continued to turn. The old ways no longer provided the answers to the current problems of the world. Did not the ancient tales and stories tell of heroes who went against the current of society? Were they not guided by the gods to accomplish their great feats, which had never before been done?

True, she was not a great general, or a demigod. She was a mortal woman, like any other, who happened to have been born to rule. But she knew the gods guided her life. She often felt their influence in the world all around her. Was it possible that they instilled within her the desire to do more with her life, while leading Ker-Ys to a brighter future at the same time?

Excitement tingled through her body at the idea. Great leaders of history did not allow the expectations or words of others to dictate their actions. As a result, they accomplished great deeds far above the limitations of ordinary people. Why not her, too? What stopped her?

Slip of a girl! Only yourself! Kenda Ptah's voice echoed in her mind.

Yes, the Atlantean was right. But how could she convince Enri to help her without marrying him? She already knew her cousin did not warm to new ideas as easily as Marcus' friend. *Maybe the idea doesn't need to be a new one?* she mused.

The guards opened the massive wooden doors leading to the great hall.

A burly man with a thick neck and light brown hair sat on a dais at the other end—Enri Loiol, leader of the Euskaldunak. To her surprise, he was quite handsome. Were it not for the ruthlessness she detected in his expression, she might have believed him a promising candidate to rule Ker-Ys with a kind hand.

Etxarte turned to her with a smile beaming on his face. "He's perfect for you," he whispered.

Marcus' tension crackled through the air. She forced herself to look at him.

He offered a nod of encouragement, though disappointment filled his eyes. *Do what you must,* they said.

His opinion means more to me than any other. How can I do without him? I cannot. It was in this moment that Gwenwhyfar realized she already held all the power needed to solve her problem.

Again, she recalled Ptah's words: *Changing your fate lies within your grasp, but only if you can prove audacious enough to seize it.*

Holding her chin high, she took a determined step forward.

MARCUS STOOD IN THE large receiving chamber that reminded him of the great hall in Ker-Ys.

In front of him, Gwenwhyfar stood with her shoulders tensed. He wanted to offer her a reassuring touch, but decided against it. *Not a good idea to give these strangers any information they may later use against us.*

At the far end of the hall, a powerful-looking man sat brooding in a chair next to the fireplace. Enri Loiol rose to greet the visitors. Tall and burly, his mere presence presented a reckoning force that filled the entire room. Judging by their harsh and unforgiving land, Marcus imagined the Vascones' reputation as a formidable people had been well earned.

Carthage wisely chose to ally with them instead of attempting to conquer them. Again, their land itself didn't strike the Roman as worth the effort of conquest. He filed that bit of information away for the future. If Carthage rose up a second time, Rome might find herself faced with enemies on multiple sides—that was, if Rome didn't make a deal with the Vascones first.

He decided the Atlanteans made a grave mistake in alienating these people. But Atlantis' mistake would prove Rome's benefit. For all their power and resources, the Atlanteans had thrown away what first made them a great people: determination and resourcefulness. These qualities projected painfully obvious in the form of this new rival who stood in the way of his happiness. His warrior's instincts deemed Gwenwhyfar's plan a brilliant one. His heart wished for anything to sabotage her designs.

But if Loiol noticed Marcus, he gave no indication of it. So had the sight of Ker-Ys' princess entranced him. "Gwenwhyfar Meur," he breathed, taking in every detail of her form. "My grandfather told me your mother was the fairest born of our people. I believed him until this moment."

Oily flatterer, Marcus thought, his jealousy mounting. Perhaps it was *they* who initiated the alliance with Carthage, and not the other way around.

Gwenwhyfar returned a graceful dip. "You honor me, cousin."

Loiol gathered his wits. "But you didn't come all this way just to hear me to shower you with praise."

Shrewd and to the point. Another mark in his favor. Marcus surmised he must have committed some forgotten, yet unforgivable sin at some point in his life. Otherwise, the gods would not punish him to this acute degree.

At last, Loiol acknowledged the presence of Gwenwhyfar's escort. "I see you brought the Romans with you. This is official, indeed."

She stepped aside to introduce the two men. "Tribune Duilius was good enough to escort us here after our mutual enemy attacked my ship."

He met the Roman's unflinching stare. "Tribune Duilius, is it?" He continued to hold Marcus' eyes, sizing him up, until he decided to resume his dialogue with Gwenwhyfar. "Why are you here?"

"I've come to heal the rift," she answered. None of her earlier apprehension showed through her non-committal mask.

He smiled thinly. "Why do you need me when you have your Roman friends?" He shot Marcus another warning look.

"I don't have the official support of Rome," she explained. "Tribune Duilius is a friend of my family."

That's a stretch. But Marcus wouldn't deny her claim.

The situation appealed to the Vascone, and he clearly believed to gain for himself the better end of whatever bargain they made.

Like unraveling a scroll, Marcus thought. *He should learn to better school his features.*

"In exchange for what?" the leader inquired.

Up to that point, Gwenwhyfar had projected an air of meekness. She now changed that demeanor, and lifted a confident brow. "Your honor."

Loiol threw back his head and laughed a loud, mocking laugh. "The approval of Ker-Ys," he scoffed.

"The reconciliation with Lord Alwyn's granddaughter," she corrected him. "His *only* granddaughter."

"And just what does Alwyn's granddaughter want in return? Our aid in your war, I suppose?"

"You suppose correctly." She patiently waited for him to mull over the proposition.

He paced back and forth a few times, weighing the pros and cons, trying to decide if the price she demanded was worth the restoration of his honor. "Alright," he growled at last, "I accept your terms. The marriage will take place tomorrow night."

Marcus felt a hole forming in the pit where his heart had sunk. But he already knew this would happen. He drained every emotion he possessed out through that hole. Only his duty remained. He might become a hollow man soon, but that was better than allowing the pain to consume him. Or worse, to allow his feelings to show in front of all.

A severe loathing of these Vascones grew up to replace the emptiness. He'd long believed his father's hatred of Carthage a loss of discipline—a rare thing for Gaius, to be sure—and he never quite understood why his father permitted the loss of control, not when every other area of his life demonstrated a model of Roman self-restraint.

Only now did the younger Duilius understand exactly what it meant to hate.

"No."

Gwenwhyfar did not raise her voice, yet the word seemed to echo throughout the hall.

Loiol blinked. Like Marcus and everyone else present, he was not certain he heard the word.

"This will not be a marriage alliance," she reiterated.

Marcus forced himself to close his mouth after his jaw nearly hit the floor.

His rival's eyes grew wide. "What sort of devilry are you trying to peddle on me, woman?"

"No devilry," she said. "I see no reason why we can't make a civilized treaty like the rest of the world."

His hands clenched into fists. "Then you can look to the rest of the civilized world to help you." He turned to leave. "This audience is over."

But Gwenwhyfar would not let this be the end. She'd come too far. "That's it? You're just going to sulk here in your hall and wallow in your dishonor? Eking out your miserable existence in this backward corner the rest of your life? Is that the sort of man you are? My grandfather was right to banish you people!"

"I will not make an agreement without blood ties!" he shouted back. "Scribbles on papyrus mean nothing! You know that!"

Feeling afraid for Gwenwhyfar's safety, Marcus grasped the hilt of his sword. *Be careful*, he wanted to tell her. *Push him too far, and he'll fight to the death to gain back his ground.* What worried him most was that he might not be able to protect her if the Vascone suddenly lashed out.

"I agree completely." She drew out her sword, passing the blade over her palm. Scarlet drops beaded along the cut. "We have reasons for our traditions," she said, holding her hand out to him.

He shook his head in disgust. "You are a woman. You cannot make this kind of alliance."

"I think you're afraid, Enri," she challenged. "You've lived so long in disgrace you think you may not measure up to a life of integrity. So you're going to take the easy way out and make excuses to cover your cowardice!"

He seethed. If looks could kill, he would have turned her to ash with his eyes.

Marcus gripped the hilt of his sword as tightly as his injured fist allowed, preparing for the conflict about to ensue. He noted only one exit to the fortress. Getting Gwenwhyfar out alive would prove a messy feat.

He exchanged glances with Etxarte. Behind him, he heard his marines bracing for the fight.

To the surprise of all, Loiol pulled out his knife, made an incision along his own palm, and grasped her hand. "As you wish, Gwenwhyfar Meur." He squeezed her hand until their mixing blood dripped to the ground. "In keeping with the traditions of our people, whichever of us produces an heir first inherits both of our kingdoms. Swear it!" He pushed her to her knees.

She visibly winced at the harshness of his grip.

Incensed, Marcus took a step forward—only to feel Etxarte catch hold of his arm. "Wait, Marcus," he whispered.

He lifted his hand to strike the elder man for daring such insolence. But he caught himself in time. No doubt, Etxarte would answer to Brutus if anything happened to him—not a prospect he envied.

Gwenwhyfar grunted under her cousin's harsh treatment. "I swear. And I return your family honor. Now you swear: death to our enemies!"

"Death to the Harappans!" He yanked her back to her feet, and raised their hands. "You are all witnesses," he announced. "The houses of Meur and Loiol are one again."

She pulled her hand from his cruel grasp and stepped away, where Etxarte tended to her wounded hand. Her guardian's opinion of what transpired was impossible to gage, but Marcus guessed he surely must disapprove of such savage treatment of his lady ward.

Loiol wrapped his own hand. "I give you fair warning," he said to her. "Whoever he is, I'm going to kill him."

Gwenwhyfar turned to face him, indignant at his allegation. "You assume I refused you for another man? It's much simpler than that: I don't wish to marry you."

"We'll see about that," he growled.

Either Gwenwhyfar did not hear his last comment, or she chose to ignore it. Whichever the case, Marcus found himself warming with a new admiration of the woman who had stolen his heart. He never imagined she'd top the bold feat she accomplished on the day they met, when she stormed into the Senate to challenge his superior all those years ago.

Until she did just that. How could he have doubted her?

"There's water at the well outside the door, where you may wash your hand," Loiol offered begrudgingly.

"Thank you, cousin." As she passed Marcus, she favored him with a bewitching smile, and beckoned him to follow her.

His pulse raced. *Cupid, you're a sly imp.*

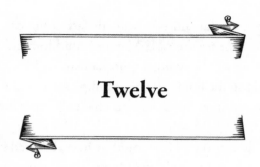

Twelve

KENDA MADE HIS WAY down the garden path toward their guest chambers behind Shahin, mulling over his theories along the way.

"Well then," remarked Shahin. "That went better than I expected."

"Worth the long trip here," Kenda scoffed, coming back to reality. "We still don't know if he will side with us."

"I think..." began the Persian.

Rounding the corner, the two men encountered a rather wide, old washer woman.

"Pardon me," said Shahin. Astonishment registered on her face. "You're Kalisada's brother!" She pointed a crooked, accusing finger in his direction. "You bear his likeness."

Shahin grasped his cloak in indignance. "Madam, you've made a mistake."

Her head bobbled from side to side. "My eyes may be old, but I'd recognize those features anywhere. They're the same features of the warrior king, the son of Lavanya, High Priestess of Kali."

Kenda laughed in her face. "Believe that to your heart's delight, old woman. It's your word against ours."

The click of her tongue matched the malice of her intent. "My word counts for more here, in the court of my king, than yours, the allegations of a foreigner."

He tugged at his earlobe in annoyance. This encounter was going to cost them. "How much do you want?" he growled, pulling out his money bag.

"All of it," she answered with a single, coy titter. She reminded Kenda of a cobra. No, cobras are much more slender than this bamboozling tub of laundry. Grumbling, he gave her the purse.

She snatched it before he had the chance to change his mind. "May you find success and fortune in all of your future lives, since this one is sadly lacking." With a wicked cackle, she disappeared down the corridor.

"Good call," Shahin said. "Exactly what you should have done."

"I'm glad you approve," he murmured.

"Someday we'll look back on this, laugh nervously, and change the subject." He gestured in the direction of the courtyard, indicating he had more to say.

Kenda complied. He guessed that more transpired during their exchange with the washerwoman than petty greed.

In the courtyard, flowering trees shaded them from the intense afternoon rays. Regardless, the heat of midday tested the endurance of most people. The sound of a trickling waterfall echoed off the stone walls. Anyone might hear their voices, though any spies must reveal themselves if they wished to distinguish their words. *No chance of the old hag overhearing our discussion*, Kenda thought with satisfaction.

"I always knew my brother's chosen path would one day haunt mine," Shahin said, dropping his nigh-constant act. "He never found the backbone to stand against his mother's demands." He shook his head. "I'd rather not have to kill him."

Kenda halted. "What's this about?" He checked his surprise, and lowered his voice. "This Kalisada can't be your brother. You're not a Harappan, you're Persian."

Shahin said nothing.

"Right?" he prodded.

"That's correct."

Kenda relaxed. "Good. For a minute there..."

"I'm *half*-Harappan. My father was a Persian ruler, and my mother a girl of Harappan descent. He also sired Kalisada, the son of my mother's sister."

Kenda tensed again.

Shahin held up his hand for silence. "Before you denounce me as a spy and betrayer, note that I left Persia and *did not* return here to India. I spent my adult life traveling the world because I never truly belonged to either of my parents' peoples."

"You could have told me."

"Had I done so, you would have reacted the same way you react now: with suspicion and prejudice."

He looked hard at Shahin. "And you expect me to trust you now, after you lied to me the entire time I've known you?"

"Technically, I haven't lied," he corrected. "You never asked me about my heritage. With a family like mine, can you blame me for a lack of eagerness about speak of my past?"

The sneak had a point, curse him. He sighed. "Does Werta know?"

Shahin picked a speck of dirt from beneath his fingernail. "He never came out and asked me, either."

The captain narrowed his eyes. "Don't think I won't tell him."

"I assumed you would," he replied stoically. "I don't intend to stop you. Right now that prospect appeals to me more than the journey leading up to my moment of reckoning. Getting out of here will not be easy, in case you haven't guessed."

Those words didn't bode well. "How can it be more difficult than it already is?" Kenda dared to ask.

Shahin leaned forward, lowering his voice further. "I don't doubt our plump 'friend' has been talking. Kalisada's spies will soon learn I am here—if they don't know already. They will pursue us until we leave these shores, and perhaps beyond. We must escape tonight before they realize we're on to them."

"Without Ashoka's leave?" Kenda gasped.

"Do you have a better idea? Besides, do you imagine he'll let us go once he learns of my lineage? Given the choice between the interests of Atlantis and our lives, I'd chose the latter. Wouldn't you?"

"Tonight," the Nubian agreed. One question lingered in his mind. "Why did you come to India if you knew they'd recognize you?"

"I did not know," he hissed. "I haven't visited here since I was a boy—I certainly don't remember that woman. The risk seemed minimal. Our situation is an unfortunate coincidence. Well, *master*," he said loud enough for the sake of any eavesdroppers present, "I bid you a pleasant sleep."

Kenda marched off to his room. Much remained for him to plan before the sun went down.

"FOR THE RECORD, I BLAME you for this."

"Me?" huffed Shahin. "This was your idea."

"Well...you should have talked me out of it! You and your brilliant schemes—bah! This particular detail will *not* go into our report, understand?"

"Rest assured, you'll find me silent as the grave on this point."

"And stop using morbid expressions!" Kenda grasped the yards of fabric that made up his skirt just before it tripped him.

They did not dare go to the king about the matter, for fear of letting the cat out of the bag regarding their plans for an early departure. Dressed as washer women, slipping past the guards proved an easy matter. Not surprising, since every one of the washer women he saw differed little from their devious blackmailer. If on guard duty himself, Kenda doubted he'd give any of the hard-featured washerwomen a second glance—not when plenty of gorgeous courtesans flitted about for men to make eyes at.

For all he knew, the very clothing he wore belonged to that conniving old bag who stole his money.

"Death and taxes! I can't believe I'm going through with this!" he uttered along with a fowl curse.

But provided their luck held out, they intended to put many miles between them and the city of Pataliputra.

AS THE SETTING SUN's rays touched their faces, they had indeed journeyed far away from Ashoka's grand capital city. Kenda hoped they might have at least until midday before the housekeepers noticed their absence. Or perhaps longer, if the king decided to keep his guests waiting as long as on the first day.

"Best keep these dresses on until get nearer to the coast," Shahin advised.

"I was afraid you'd say that."

Shahin dismissed the remark. His suggestion was likely his revenge for Kenda's idea of dressing in drag in order to escape from the palace undetected. But neither had been able to contrive a better plan. "I suggest we make for Tamralipiti rather than Tosali."

"But our ship is waiting at Tosali—no, you're right," he realized. "They'll send the assassins there first."

"We can follow this river." Shahin stopped abruptly on the banks of the waterway.

Kenda had not even seen it until he ran into the Persian's back. "It's a more direct route, if memory serves. Easier when one wishes to keep off the roads, in any case. Once in Tamralipiti, we can obtain passage back home."

"As deckhands—or worse, rowers." Kenda groaned. He pressed his palm to his forehead. "How do I get roped into these situations?"

"I don't plan to add either of those skills to my list of work experience," Shahin assured him. "Our fat friend was too busy gloating over her discovery of my identity to take *my* money. What I have left should buy us both passage, so long as we practice thrift."

THAT NIGHT, KENDA FOUND himself in a tree just outside the city of Champa, where they meant to sleep.

"What about snakes?" he inquired.

Shahin rattled the branches.

Kenda barely got a grip on his branch in time to keep from falling. Several slithering serpents dropped to the ground. Kenda was certain his skin lightened several shades. Mercifully, it was too dark for his companion to see it.

"They probably won't bother to climb back up tonight," said Shahin.

"Probably? Or won't? There's a distinct difference."

He shrugged. "I'm not sleeping on the ground. You are free to make your own decisions."

Kenda scrutinized each branch near his own, but found nothing. With string of inane protests, he leaned back against the trunk. This was ridiculous! Captains of the Atlantean Navy did not fear crawling creatures. Crossing his arms over his chest, he closed his eyes and willed himself into a restless doze.

He awoke at the crack of dawn, eager to climb down from that tree and its slinking residents. He shook his associate's branch. "Time to go."

Shahin yawned and opened his eyes. "Good morning, captain. I see the assassins have failed again."

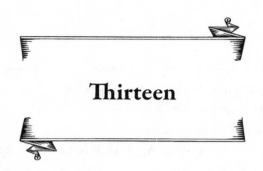

Thirteen

MARCUS FELT NUMB ALL over, hardly noticing the chilled air of the alleyway as it hit him.

Even after witnessing it transpire in front of him, he still had trouble believing what Gwenwhyfar had done, what she'd sacrificed for him. He watched her wash at the well further down the narrow alley, taking in every detail of her lovely form.

She loved him—she *must* love him! All his hopes, dreams, and desires found a new life, demonstrating how fortunes could change in but an instant.

Gwenwhyfar loved him! Enri Loiol, Prince of the Euskaldunak, held the power to solve all of Ker-Ys' problems. Yet Gwenwhyfar instead chose him, Marcus Duilius, a plebeian turned war hero.

He savored the revelation, allowing its glorious sweetness to wash over him. Every trial, every obstacle—it had all been worth what he endured. He would win the woman he loved—he believed that now without any doubt.

At his side, the marine cleared his throat, "Sir." He tilted his head toward the door, indicating another person approached.

Etxarte stormed out the doorway. "The girl's out of her mind! This is your doing, isn't it?" he accused, pointing a finger at Marcus. "No good will come of this!"

Gwenwhyfar paused at her guardian's words, but made no attempt to engage in the discussion. She went back to cleaning her injured hand.

Marcus straightened his back. "I can honestly tell you I had nothing to do with it. She's quite capable of conjuring up these schemes on her own. You should understand that better than I."

"Ha! If only I did!" He continued as though she wasn't there. "She used to run off into the forest on her own with her scrolls. I spent hours searching for her, fearing the entire time that she was being mauled by wild boars or wolves. When I finally found her, she'd proudly recite some poem or historical chronicle she'd memorized—heedless of the anguish that struck my heart on her account," he added in her direction.

"Children seldom do," Marcus offered. "Just ask my mother."

To that point, Etxarte had no response. "Don't make the mistake of assuming this means she's available for you now. Because she isn't."

Marcus offered a shrug of feigned innocence. Etxarte left in a huff.

THE FRIGID WATER STUNG into the open wound on her palm. Gwenwhyfar's hand went numb with continued contact with the water. The bleeding stopped, and she proceeded to wrap her hand with clean linen. She felt grateful she possessed the wherewithal to seal their bargain with her left hand rather than her dominant right.

Over and over again, she asked herself if she'd only made another mistake. And yet, the moment she saw Enri, she could not bring herself to enter into a marriage of state with him. He was not a Valens Petronius. A strange—dare she think it, otherworldly—cruelty lurked in her cousin's eyes. From the time she crossed his threshold, Enri already looked on her as his own—his chattel, to do with as he pleased. He would view her people in a similar manner, were he to rule them.

No. She had taken the right course.

She squinted down at her reflection rippling in the bottom of the well. The right thing had turned into another gamble. Enri might yet still rule Ker-Ys. But surely, far better for a possessive Euskaldunak lord to rule her people than some Harappan destroyer? If she could prevent either outcome, all the better.

Marcus' reflection rippled beside her. She started, and dropped the bucket down into the cistern.

He caught her in his arms and pulled her close. "Don't fall."

Her stomach fluttered with butterflies. Her knees buckled.

"You're quite a woman, Gwenwhyfar," he said, in awe. "Just when I think I've figured you out, you blow me out of the water once more with your capabilities." He brushed a rogue curl out of her face. "I think you'll always remain a mystery to me. The most wonderful mystery of my life."

"A girl does what she must," she replied with a coy smile, tracing the design on his breastplate. She knew she should pull away from him right that instant, before one of Enri's people saw them.

"I'll never love any other woman but you," he promised. "How can I, when no other woman can possibly compare?"

He drew her lips into an ardent kiss, his unshaven chin gently scratching her skin. His touch was so tender, so loving, yet at the same time strong and confident. He adored her.

She wanted to surrender to his kisses forever, to be his wife, to belong to him.

Why was it she could never resist Marcus Duilius? She didn't *wish* to resist him— there lied the problem.

She forced herself to step apart from him. "Marcus, please. Someone might see."

He coaxed her back. "I don't care if they do. Bring them on. I'll fight them all with my bare hands if it means winning you." He clenched his fist as though it settled the matter.

"You need to improve you skills in diplomacy, tribune," she scolded, though she did not deny she liked the idea of him fighting for love of her. She adored the way he always tried to impress her.

Quite smitten, Marcus did not take her chiding seriously. "I won't disappoint you, my brave, beautiful Gwenwhyfar. I'm not ignorant of what you've done for me."

"Aren't you?" She searched his handsome, dark eyes.

He brought her injured hand to his lips. "You've put your birthright as ruler of KerYs in jeopardy. Because you want a life with me." He nuzzled his face in her hand. "You shouldn't have done that, but I'm happy beyond words that you did. I've stood at the jaws of death itself without fear countless times. And yet, I don't know how I could endure it if you married him. I know, it's selfish of me."

"No," she sighed. "I'm the selfish one. I put the desires of my heart ahead of my responsibilities. My people may suffer for it."

He lifted her chin and looked her in the eye. "They won't. Regardless of who inherits, you are both capable leaders. I'll concede to Loiol on that point. Besides," he added with a sultry smirk, "I wouldn't give up on heirs just yet."

She playfully slapped his hand away. Only then did she notice the bruises on his knuckles. "How long has your hand been like this?" she gasped.

"What, that?" He dismissed the injury. "It's nothing."

"Marcus! How did it happen?"

"I punched a wall," he confessed. "I was angry. I thought I'd lost you." He took her into his arms again. "Say you love me, Gwenwhyfar. I must hear it."

"I love you," she said, her skin skin tingling at his touch.

He nuzzled his forehead to hers. "That's all I need to hear, and I'll do anything for you, my beautiful princess."

She took the roll of bandages to wrap his hand.

He stopped her. "I still intend to ask you to marry me when the war is over."

"I'm still waiting for you to ask," she returned sweetly.

"I will," he promised, "at the earliest opportunity."

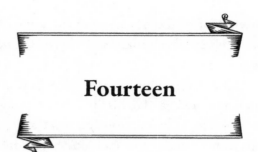

Fourteen

LOIOL TOOK THEM ON a tour of his fortress, since the obligation now fell on him to trust his visitors.

"As you can see," he boasted, gesturing across the length of the walls, "we have supplies enough to feed our people for many years, if necessary. Here in our stronghold, we will outlast the Harappans. To the south lies the training ground, and housing for our elephants."

"Have you fought the Harappans yourself?" asked Marcus.

For the sake of Gwenwhyfar's presence, he tried to keep the challenge out of his tone. The Vascone had lost the first battle, but Marcus knew better than to assume he'd given up on the war. Loiol dropped his arm.

"No," he admitted. "Since you possess such a great military prowess, perhaps you'd care to assess our strengths? I'd love to have the opinion of a Roman. In the interests of our newfound friendship, of course."

You mean, for when you fight Rome again, Marcus wanted to say. "Of course," he echoed, his tone barely civil.

Loiol forced an expression of false pleasure. "I have an idea." He took Gwenwhyfar's hand. "I realize I've behaved as a beast to you, cousin. Will you let me make it up to you?"

Marcus wanted to gag. *And I thought Stigandr was an eel.*

She pulled her hand away in a slow, dignified motion. "Very well."

"You're anxious to get back to Ker-Ys, but please stay tonight for dinner and a night's rest before your grueling voyage in a cramped trireme."

"That's generous of you," she said.

Marcus forced down his annoyance at the idea that their "host" hadn't offered any gestures of hospitality before. Had he intended to send them back to the ship for the night? He decided against telling him they had no ship to return to at the moment, and he hoped Gwenwhyfar possessed the foresight enough to play along.

"At dinner, I wish to present you with a few gifts." He sent a boyish pout in her direction, trying to endear himself to her. "I had hoped them to be wedding gifts..."

She raised a brow and folded her arms, unmoved.

"...but, you may have them anyway," he finished. "No conditions. Only reminders that my offer still stands, should you change your mind. Or, tokens of peace. You may choose the reason."

"Tokens of peace will do just fine," she said.

"As you wish." He bit his lip. "Can you blame me for trying when I have such beauty to tempt me?" He clapped his hands, and two female servants appeared. "See to it that Lady Gwenwhyfar is refreshed for dinner tonight. She is to be given every luxury, and anything else she asks for."

He turned back to his guests. "I think you'll find, cousin, that we are not entirely uncivilized here. Please excuse the tribune and I while we tour the fortress and surrounding land works." He held up his hand before she could object. "I'll send a messenger to report everything to you later on. I give you my word."

Gwenwhyfar admitted to some fatigue, and allowed the servants to lead her away.

"Now then." He grasped his hands together. "What would you care to see first, tribune? The earthworks, perhaps?"

"Fine." Marcus did not care. But he felt easier now that Loiol's roving eye no longer fixed on Gwenwhyfar. Instead, he was right where Marcus could keep his eye on him. The snake was up to something—he could feel it. Their host suggested that they first try out the elephants, no doubt intending to watch Marcus make a fool of himself by his lack of skill in controlling the imposing animals. But the Roman noticed that the cavalry stables stood much closer, and pointed out they'd have more time to inspect the defenses if they chose horses instead.

They rode down into the valley below, to the trenches at the edge of the forest. High on the bluff above, the imposing fortress of the Vascones stood, guarding the pass into the mountains.

He had to admit, they held their defenses well, and he could offer few suggestions for improvement. But that didn't stop him from filing away the weaknesses he did see for when the day came when he might need take this fortress with his future legions.

No, Gwenwhyfar wouldn't approve of that, he surmised. *Though she may change her mind when she learns the full truth of her cousin's deception.* "Extend this trench farther north," he recommended. "In Ker-Ys, we flooded some of the trenches with seawater. Your cousin approved of this method, and it helped save the city."

"She doesn't care what you think," Loiol averred.

The bluntness of the remark caught him off guard, and his comeback carried a more smug tone than he intended to allow. "I doubt that."

The Vascone fell silent, and they rode on to the forest's edge. He continued to hold his tongue when they arrived. Lowering himself from his horse, he took a drink of water from the babbling brook. What sly scheme brewed in his mind?

Marcus kept his guard up, ready for the beast to pounce on him at any moment. "Is there a spring within the fortress walls? The enemy might easily poison this one."

"I know that," Loiol growled. "Yes, there's a water source."

A not-so-silent sigh, and Marcus dismounted. When he raised his head, he found himself staring down the length of a sword. "I came here in good faith! I was told I could trust your word."

Loiol laughed, presumably the first genuine expression since they met that morning. "That's what you get for relying on a woman's judgment. I didn't know you Romans were so soft. Your people didn't display any tenderheartedness when you executed my father for his ties to Carthage."

Marcus wrinkled his nose. "That's what happens when you choose the wrong allies. So you intend to betray Gwenwhyfar, too?"

"No. But I do intend to marry her." His devious grin fell into a hard frown. "And you're standing in my way."

"Me?" he feigned.

Did Loiol overheard their conversation at the well? His spies might have. Gwenwhyfar was right in advising caution. Why did he not heed her?

"She didn't contrive that little scheme on her own. It was a bit too...Roman."

Marcus snorted. "You think that idea came from me? I know nothing of your customs. Believe me, right up until that stunt, I thought she was going to marry you as much as you did."

"I don't believe you," he quipped. "I'm going to kill you. Now, I suggest you pray to whatever gods you Romans like to worship."

"You think she won't find out you murdered me? Don't underestimate her, it will be your undoing." He hoped she might somehow chance to peer out of a window from the castle above in time to witness her cousin's betrayal.

"You're supposed to be praying!" he snarled. "On your knees, pig."

Marcus complied. "You don't want to kill me, Loiol."

"Oh, I think I do." He raised the blade to slit Marcus' throat. Then, with an exasperated groan, he lowered it. "Alright, why don't I want to kill you?"

A good question. Marcus was not sure when he uttered the desperate claim that his enemy would sniff the bait. He had to think fast.

"Because," he began slowly, "she'll never marry you if you do. You won't be able to hide this from her. She's not stupid. If I truly am the reason she won't marry you, as you claim, she'll hate you forever. You'll never woo her—and you must woo her, if you wish to rule Ker-Ys."

A weak argument, he owned, but with luck it would win him the time he needed. That Loiol still hesitated told Marcus he'd hit the mark at the dead center.

"I don't need her to rule Ker-Ys," he barked. "I can find any woman to produce my heir before she does."

"Why don't you, then? Unless it's you who's gone soft? A man with your ambitions doesn't let a woman's whims ruin his plans."

The look on Loiol's face might have stopped a raging elephant in its tracks. Only then did Marcus realize he'd gone too far.

"You're right. He doesn't. That's why I've decided to kill you after all."

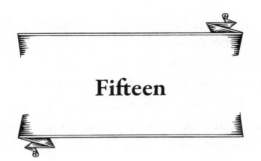

Fifteen

"DEAD? WHAT DO YOU MEAN, 'dead'?" Werta slammed the report down on his desk.

His secretary stood already prepared for his reaction. "For what it's worth, the captain likewise has his doubts about Ashoka's claim of 'an unfortunate accident.'"

"Why didn't he *do* something? All the gods and Hades!"

She brushed a blonde curl over her shoulder. "What could he do? Protocol dictates he couldn't leave his ship until he returned here. And he hadn't the means to issue his own investigation. As it is, he got flack from every port master since Tosali because he waited for news of them as long as he did."

Werta went over to the window in a huff. Down in the streets below, Atlanteans bustled about the city, heedless of his problems. "I've sent other men and women to their deaths before, you know. But this...this is different."

"Because you had no reason to think they would not come back," she offered, struggling to maintain a professional detachment.

"Yes, I believe that's it. Exactly. And no matter what any one says about Shahin, I know the man. He was trying to go straight. Why are people punished for doing the right thing?"

"King Ashoka apologizes profusely, and has sent us gifts along with the hope that," she glanced down at her copy of the message, "'this unfortunate accident will not damage the promising beginning of a lasting friendship between our nations, the hope which both he and the late Ambassador Ptah shared.'"

He dismissed the explanation with a wave. "Yes, yes, I can see that. Past operatives have reported Ashoka demonstrates a genuine desire for peace. Based on that information, I don't think he's responsible."

"But," she interjected, "he might look the other way, if doing so were in his best interests. Or to avoid confrontations with his neighbors on their account."

"My thoughts exactly." He sank into his chair and pinched the bridge of his nose. "Send out copies of the report to the Council. And go away. I need some time alone to think. Don't go away angry, just go away."

Werta closed his eyes and focused on the babbling waterfalls of the small fishpond in his office. The sound of running water had a way of relaxing a person —a reason Atlanteans used waterclocks to note the passage of time instead of stress-inducing mechanical devices. If he listened closely enough, he could hear the fish splashing as they darted about.

He did not believe Ashoka's report for a second. Ptah and Shahin remained alive—and likely, in trouble. He could not put his finger on it, but something didn't feel quite right. From what he knew of Ashoka thus far, the man was not some apathetic leader. He calculated everything well in advance before he acted.

Unfortunately, the power to wait did not rest with Atlantis' mayor. The Council decided those matters. Given the way the political winds blew of late, coupled with the itchy trigger fingers among the military leaders, they would choose to act rather than wait.

His brow hardened with determination. "Death and taxes! If the time we need is not afforded to us, I'll *make* the time."

MARCUS GLARED UP AT Loiol from his knees, uttering a curse which indicated in no uncertain terms his exact opinion of his rival.

Loiol smirked. "Ah, Roman directness. That's one thing I'll concede to admiring about your people. Your language is so...expressive."

"You'll regret this vile deception," the tribune vowed.

"Not as much as you do, I think," the Vascone quipped. "Don't worry, Gwenwhyfar will be in good hands. Around here, we like to keep things," he added an evil smile for emphasis, "in the family."

"That's sickening."

Loiol raised his sword to strike. "Goodbye, Tribune Marcus Duilius. Or, as your people like to say, *Vale—*"

"What in the netherworld do you think you are you doing, boy?" a voice boomed through the valley.

Etxarte stood up on his horse's stirrups, his furious expression demanding an explanation.

Loiol lowered the sword and whirled around to face the man who had dared to interrupt the execution. "I am not 'boy,'" he seethed, "I'm the Lord of the Euskaldunak!"

"This is an outrage!" he yelled, dismissing the younger man's claims. "The Loiols have been many things down through the ages. But I never thought a snake in the grass was one of them—until now. Your grandfather would be ashamed of you! My only consolation is that he can't see you now."

"Mind you own business, old coot!"

Marcus was not sure which he loathed more, the thought of Etxarte rescuing him from the *paterfamilias* of all eels, or that this kettle of fish had boiled over into one disgusting mess. Either reason was enough to justify following through with the idea that entered his mind.

He chose the first reason, mainly because he'd cleaned up worse messes in his service to the Republic.

Rising to his feet, he gave his attacker a jovial punch in the shoulder. "Looks like you've bested me, my friend. I'll make sure to add that maneuver to my new training regimen."

Loiol's face grew red with humiliation. Marcus reveled in each deepening shade of it.

Like a good dog, he took the way out offered to him. "It's the least I can do, tribune," he ground out, "since you were generous enough to advise me on my earthworks."

Etxarte eyed the pair. "Do you expect me to swallow that hogwash?"

"I know, right?" Marcus laughed. "We Romans pride ourselves in training the best military in the world. And this fellow from the mountains brought me to my knees before I could blink an eye. But, I know I can count on my friends to keep this little embarrassment a secret—especially from a certain pair of lovely ears?"

The captain gawked from Marcus to Loiol.

"I am as silent as the grave," the lord oiled.

There's a good dog, Marcus thought. *Chew your bone well—it's the only one you'll get.*

"Fine," said Etxarte. "But you're going to have to prove your loyalty to me, because I'm not going to forget about this. *Boy*. And you," he pointed to Marcus. "This changes nothing."

The Roman mounted his mare with a grunt of satisfaction. "I expect not." Right before he spurred her on, he added over his shoulder, "Oh, and Loiol, don't forget about that stream there. Wouldn't want you to lose men to an irksome demise like poison. True, that's more of a feminine strategy. But we can't always count on our enemies to conduct themselves as real men, can we?"

Enri glared back.

Marcus eased his horse off into a cantor back to the fortress, chuckling.

Etxarte caught up to him a few minutes later.

"I suppose I owe you my thanks," said the tribune.

"Yes, you do. But don't get used to it. And another thing: stop getting into fights over her. Because next time, I have no intention of saving your worthless hide."

"I'll try to remember that," he said. "Still disappointed she's not going to marry him?"

The Vascone brought his horse to a halt. "That's not any of your business." Then his tone mellowed. "Allowing him to save face, that was noble of you, and I thank you for it. But don't get any ideas. You're still not suitable for her."

The Roman nodded, and kicked his mare into a full, jubilant gallop. Gwenwhyfar's stern and immovable guardian considered him noble!

A small concession, true, but Marcus would take it.

FOR MONTHS, ADMIRAL Itza had wanted action. He entreated for the power to rid Atlantis of her enemies forever. Ever since they lost most of the force sent to aid Ker-Ys, he did not cease in his clamors for a preemptive strike against the Harappans in the heart of their territory.

"Destroy the hornets' nest, and they'll stop coming to sting you," became his motto.

"I lament Ptah's loss," he said, "both as a comrade and a friend. But we can't let our personal feelings cloud our judgment." He wore the blue and silver armor of an Atlantean admiral. In his shoulder-length black hair, he also bore Mayan feathers to remind him of his Western roots. "How long have I said we can't just sit here and do nothing while these barbarians raid the lands around us? Our list of allies grows shorter, Werta—they're dropping like flies!"

"We have no clue where their nest lies," the mayor countered.

A major piece to this puzzle yet eluded them. Every bone in Werta's body told him so. The warhawks continued squawking all around him, pushing for action. Yet he sensed that if they moved too soon without the critical information Ptah and Shahin would surely bring, they would make some fatal, irretrievable error.

He must find a way to placate the warmongers, to stall them and give enough time for their operatives to return. But how?

"Are we going to stand here and idly let the murder of our comrades go unavenged?" asked Itza.

Nax, one of the Council elders, spoke up, leaning on his cane. "I agree with all that has been said. The time has indeed come for action. But I also agree with Mayor Werta. It is unwise to act rashly without a plan."

"No situation is ever perfect," countered Itza. "The longer we wait for 'the right time,' the more we get stung. I for one have had enough of these meddling insects."

While the others present in the council chamber squabbled, Werta's mind traveled outside of the window, past the city, and off toward the open sea. Fishermen's boats dotted the horizon.

What a simple life those men must enjoy, he mused. Not prestigious by any stretch of the imagination, but oh, so blissfully uncomplicated!

His ancestors started out in Atlantis as fishermen. His great-great grandfather strove long and hard to break the barrier of his family's limited social mobility. If he could see Werta today, he would surely smile with pride that his labors had borne the fruit he coveted.

The life of an insignificant fisherman. At the moment, it seemed to him preferable to Mayor of Atlantis. He pictured himself working with his hands, enjoying the simple life, hauling nets of fish into a boat all day.

Loads of fish... Say, now there's an idea!

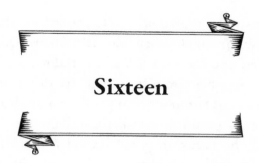

Sixteen

FORTY-FIVE MINUTES ago, their cover had been blown. They'd succeeded in eluding the assassins for the first three days.

But the spies caught up to them just south of the city of Champa. Their good fortune up to that point lured them into a false sense of security. When that happened, even the mightiest warriors might fall victim to an ambush.

One of the attackers had his arm around Shahin's neck, poising to snap his spine like a twig. Kenda was by far the better fighter, but his own trio of goons to kept him busy. They were not exceptionally good, but when three went against one, the odds seldom added up in the single person's favor.

By some stroke of luck, he managed to fell his adversaries in time to come to Shahin's aid. With no small amount of apprehension, he inspected the dead warriors lying on the ground around them. Nothing on or about them shed any light in regards to their affiliation. But that did not surprise him. He assumed Kalisada's agents hired them, and they took the assignment not knowing their targets' significance.

Shahin blinked at him, still wheezing to get his breath back. "You're not dead."

"No," Kenda grunted.

"Congratulations." After a moment passed, he added, "Thank you for saving my life."

"Don't get used to it."

The next two days proved uneventful, aside from their occasional swiping a tray of cooling samosas left unguarded on kitchen windowsills here and there. Ptah loathed stealing, even if it was the only thing keeping them from starvation. Yet they had little choice. Shahin's money must last in order to pay for passage back to Atlantis. Foraged fruit alone would not sustain them all the way to the coast.

At one of the farms, they hid behind a tree while an angry grandmother scolded her grandson for gobbling up the family's dinner. No matter how vehemently the boy claimed his innocence, she refused to believe him, and informed him that his father would spank him when he came home.

Kenda clenched his fists, feeling remorseful that his belly was chalk full of the confounded samosas. "I hate cowering here while an innocent boy has to pay for our crimes."

"It will build his character." Shahin swallowed his last bite and licked his fingers. "He'll grow up a stronger man because of it. Don't worry about him."

He'll grow up like you, Kenda bit back.

Anytime they encountered people, he let Shahin do the talking, and that was only when they could not avoid people altogether. His foreign appearance concerned him. His skin was much darker than the locals, and spies on the lookout for them would pick him out immediately. Shahin, on the other hand, might at least blend into a crowd, even with his infamous family ties.

On the seventh day after beating their hasty retreat from Ashoka's palace, they traveled nearer to the edge of a great river, just along the jungle's border. Shahin stopped in front of a stone marker intricately carved in the shape of a hideous sea monster.

"Ah," he remarked. "That's more like it."

Kenda regarded the statue's exuberant coils. "What *is* that obscene beast?"

"He's Vasuki, a serpent king. Legend has it, he churned up the sea in search of the elixir of immortality submerged in the depths. It means we're near the coast."

The Nubian's heart lightened. "That's more like it."

"If you'll excuse me," said Shahin, "I'm going to relieve myself." He wandered off and disappeared into the lush foliage.

"Hurry up. And don't stop to examine any more statues. I want to get going."

The sooner they left this inhospitable land, the better. Shahin may find all of this art and culture fascinating, but Kenda thought it demented and disturbing—the stuff that made up his worst nightmares. More than anything, he longed to get back to familiar, logical Atlantis.

Squatting down to wash the road's dust from his face, he saw the reflection of a young girl in the rippling water.

"Good day to you, stranger," she said in merchants' Greek. "You're not from around here."

"No," he admitted, looking up at her.

He considered himself an experienced judge of character, and though she was a pretty little chick, he perceived right away there was something about her he didn't like.

"I am not a threat to you," she giggled, "Mister...Aksumite?"

Close enough. He'd rather she did not know his exact origins. He did not offer his name, either. "I see you're an educated girl."

She dipped her water pots into the bubbling river. "Not really. I'm a traveler. My family travels the lands to trade in silk and other cloths. I see many things and many peoples. My name is Chandra. We're on our way to Tamralipiti. Would you like to travel with us?"

"I'm waiting for someone."

Just in time, Shahin appeared and saw her.

"Oh, hello," she said. "You must be Mr. Aksumite's friend. I was just offering a place in our caravan for the two of you, if you are also headed in the direction of Tamralipiti?"

The two men exchanged glances. Shahin offered no suggestions.

"We have no interest in political affairs," she assured them, "only in trade. You'll be quite safe with us. Safer than traveling through these jungles alone, I'll wager. This is tiger country, you know."

Kenda looked sideways at Shahin. *Thanks for warning me ahead of time.* "We haven't decided where we're going yet. But we'll consider your offer. Thank you."

"Our camp lies just above the ravine over there," she pointed the way, "should you change your mind. We depart in an hour." With a friendly smile, she left, balancing one of the water pots on her head and carrying the other on her hip.

"I didn't see her approach," Kenda explained, once she was out of earshot.

"No matter," said Shahin. "I think we should take her up on her offer."

"You're joking."

"I'm not. It's true that traders have few, if any, political aims. What's more, a man with obvious African features looks less conspicuous in a group like theirs rather than traveling on his own in this country."

"A valid point," Kenda conceded. "We can't expect not to run into more pursuers. I suppose I'm more concerned about them talking if the authorities start asking them questions."

"They're more likely to mention that they saw us if we *aren't* traveling with them," Shahin pointed out.

"Fine," Kenda agreed. "But I don't trust her."

"You're wise not to. Remind me to tell you a story I once heard about a woman named Delilah." He splashed his hands in the water. "We must continue to practice vigilance, and watch each other's backs at all times. The danger is by no means lessened now, only of a different kind."

THE SPEAKER OF THE House leaned on the podium for emphasis. "Councilpersons, I urge you: We must strike them—before they strike us. You all know the Harappans' intentions. These bloodthirsty savages are our enemy, and they intend to attack our fair Atlantis. Please, don't let Captain Ptah's heroic sacrifice go wasted, or his vile murder unavenged. Your vote will decide the future of our children, and their children—and beyond. Remember that. Thank you."

The deliberations over, the Council members rose to begin the process casting their votes.

"Madam Speaker," Werta piped up, "before the vote is cast, I have a few things to add."

She returned a wintry smile. "As Mayor, that is your right, of course. You may address the Council. The Council recognizes Mayor Nedril Werta, who claims the Mayor's Right of Statement," she barked to the scribes.

Werta came already prepared. "Thank you for sharing the podium, Madam Speaker."

Stepping onto the floor, he unrolled one of the scrolls he'd nonchalantly carried into the session under his arm. "Councilpersons: You've all made valid contributions to this debate. As you are already aware, I think this course of action is too hasty. We *do* have to consider how a war will affect future generations. These are matters that cannot be rushed.

"Let me give you an example. Did you know it takes *garum* on average between twenty-seven and sixty-two days to ferment to perfection? Rush the process, and you end up with a bucket of rotten fish goo. Personally, I prefer to let mine sit in the sun for closer to seventy days. But everyone has their own way of preparing it. To me, the factory-produced stuff simply won't do."

The politicians shifted in their seats as his purpose dawned on them.

With an amusement that bordered on the perverse, he dived right into his lecture. "Now, my mother and grandmother always disagreed on exactly how high one should fill the barrel—and I could tell the difference between the two recipes. Things got even more heated when my aunts and uncles ventured their own opinions. I like both variations equally, mind you—don't want to open that can of worms again," he chuckled. "I'd rather stick with our proverbial fine kettle of fish."

A collective groan resonated through the council chamber at the lousy attempt at humor.

Before he finished his filibuster, he held every confidence the entire Council would know how to make *garum* from memory. Perhaps some of them would even think of how to create their own variations from his mother's recipes out of sheer boredom.

"You wouldn't think a little thing like that would matter, but trust me: it does. Of course, I have my own theory as to why that happens, and I'm happy to have the opportunity to share it with you all..."

It was going to be a long, miserable session. Werta hoped against hope his efforts would not prove in vain.

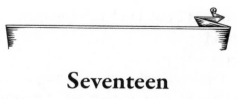

Seventeen

SHE WAS A WONDERFUL liar, that girl Chandra. The instant Kenda set his eyes on her, he saw her for what she truly was: a deceitful little bird, full of wicked wiles.

But did she mean them any physical harm? He must assess the danger and decide what to do—and do it quickly before they found themselves backed into a corner.

The girl gestured toward the pot of soup over the fire. "Please, share a meal with us. It is but simple fare, but all that is ours is yours."

"Thank you," he answered. But he waited before taking any. Shahin hesitated, too. *My suspicions are not unfounded after all.*

"Something wrong?" she inquired sweetly.

"Ah, please excuse my manners, which must come across as quite strange to you. In Aksum, the hostess is always served first."

"A strange custom," she mused. She looked to Shahin. "I've eaten with Persians before, and they didn't follow that practice."

Shahin had stared into the flickering flames of the campfire for most of the evening, still torn over what to do about his relations. "I follow the ways of my master," he said, only half out of his reverie.

Chandra shook her head, causing her earrings to jingle. "If that is your wish." She filled her bowl and sipped the warm liquid. She seemed so dainty and innocent.

But Kenda knew better. She hid something, and he hoped Shahin possessed the wits to see it, too. In the meantime, she ate through half the bowl. So the soup was safe enough. On the other hand, the possibility existed that Chandra and the others may have swallowed the antidote beforehand.

Or, maybe he was just paranoid.

His stomach rumbled, loud enough for everyone to hear. He could no longer present any more excuses without arousing his hosts' suspicions. He scooped some soup into his bowl, inhaling the spicy aroma with relish. Shahin followed.

"It's delicious," he said after a few mouthfuls. And it was. He eased his worries by reminding himself that most poisons tasted bitter, which was why assassins often chose wine. Given the amount of spices in Indian cooking, however, he considered a bitter taste might be concealed.

I've been on the run too long.

Not much to do about it now. He'd already eaten it, and may as well enjoy the experience, since another hot meal may not come along again in a while. Once they got back to sea, hardened biscuits and salted fish would keep them alive all the way to Atlantis.

Cheerful thought. He helped himself to another bowl.

Chandra's face shined. "You like it? I'm so glad."

Something in her lovely face tossed all of his reassurances out the window. He offered a polite dip of his head in response, and swallowed down the liquid with a hard gulp.

After all ate their fill, the travelers lay down upon their spread blankets and closed their eyes. Kenda made a visual sweep all around him.

"The fire will keep away most snakes," Shahin whispered. "Just don't lay on the bare ground. Spread out your cloak." He followed his suggestion with a wink.

Kenda caught his guide's meaning right away: don't go to sleep. As he suspected all along, something indeed was afoot.

Chandra produced a flute from her sack of belongings. "Allow me to play for you." She didn't wait for an answer, but began her soft trilling. Her relatives mumbled their approval.

Kenda lay back and stared up at the moonless sky. The stars twinkled above as Chandra's haunting melody floated on the cool night breeze. He closed his eyes and pretended to doze. He didn't dare allow himself to be lulled to sleep on this night. To do so would surely cost him his life.

No matter how hard he tried, he couldn't ignore the sound of the flute.

The beautiful music was like a magic, melting away his weariness and cares, piquing his curiosity about this enigmatic land and its people. The soul of India itself seemed to dwell in her song, and he felt a longing in his heart for this place, which before then he had never visited. Now that he caught a glimpse of its mystery, he felt certain this desire would never cease.

India would always be a part of him.

THE NEXT THING HE KNEW, he perceived a pain piercing his arm. It felt dull at first, then as he came to, it sharpened.

Voices. Chandra's flute had long ceased. Instead, he heard her voice mingled with the others in a low, wanton chanting.

He had permitted the unthinkable: he fell asleep.

His eyes opened, and he saw them dancing around the fire in a trance-like state.

"Shh!" someone said in his ear—Shahin. "Don't let them see you're awake."

Kenda tried to bring his hands in front, but his arms met resistance. To his horror, he understood his wrists were tied behind him. *How could I have let this happen? There* was *a drug in the soup. What a fool I am!*

The "merchants" stopped their dancing and gathered in a circle. One of them unwrapped a cloth filled with tiny cakes colored in red dye, and passed them around. Raising the cakes to the air, they ate them in one bite.

The tuneless chorus and wild gyrating resumed, mounting into a crescendo. "Kali...Kali...!" they chanted, whirling their scarves around.

If he believed in any gods, Kenda would have sworn at every single one of them. He and Shahin had wandered into a nest of Harappans!

Why didn't he recognize them before? Had his memories of endless rowing in the misery of their galley faded from his mind so soon?

He heard a muffled snap from Shahin's direction. "I'm free. I'll release you soon as they turn again. Then we run hard and don't look back."

Kenda nodded eagerly. How wrong he was to think Shahin had lost his wits! Whatever else he was or had done, the reformed half-Harappan saved his life. He resolved to reconsider his opinion of the man once they escaped from this nightmare.

But in one, awful instant his hopes were dashed, for Chandra turned and caught his open eyes. She shrieked the alarm.

The spell broke with a jolt. All eyes turned to the prisoners.

Shahin sprung to his feet, pulling Kenda up with him. He cut the bonds with a single, fluid movement. He didn't have to remind him to run.

Dew-covered brush and leaves whipped around them, smacking them in their faces as they raced deep into the jungle. Firelight from their pursuers' torches cast tall shadows through the trees.

They were gaining, and he realized he'd lost sight of Shahin in the darkness. He did not dare call out to him, lest their hunters hear. *The fleas of a thousand camels infest him, the sneak! So much for changing my opinion!*

He ran past a tree, where a pair of arms seized him. He barely contained a yelp of surprise.

"Up here," Shahin whistled softly.

Dashing up the tree at a speed that astonished even himself, he molded his body to the contours of the branches. They held their breath, and waited.

"Find them!" Chandra shrilled. She transformed from a sweet girl to a gorgon out for blood.

Her goons rushed past them.

Kenda leaned against the tree, breathing heavily, hoping any snakes would keep to themselves and out of his clothing. He did not know how long he froze there, but it felt like most of the night passed before monkey chatter returned to the wood.

Shahin recovered first. He dropped to the ground with the stealth of a tiger.

Tigers! Kenda had forgotten about them. Was everything and everyone in India out to get him?

"And they didn't even offer us the *ghoor*," said Shahin, dusting off his tunic. "Humph! I find that insulting."

"What's *ghoor*?" Kenda asked, once he found his voice.

"The sacred sugar of Kali, baked into bread. Partaking of it seals their pact with the goddess, while its magical qualities give her followers their impressive abilities." In the darkness, one could just make out his lecturing smirk.

"Insulting? I wouldn't participate in that disgusting ritual."

Shahin shrugged. "Nor would I, unless it served to buy us time. But they could have at least offered. That they didn't shows they never took us seriously to start with. That is what offends me."

"That was their mistake," said Kenda. "I'm sure they're berating themselves over their lack of foresight as we speak. Console yourself with that."

"I shall. And while we gloat, we should move along before Kali inspires them to retrace their steps."

"Ridiculous superstition," Ptah scoffed. "But I agree, we should get going."

In the darkness of that foreign wilderness, any business involving the blood goddess gave Kenda a chilling fright, though he would never admit it.

Strange enough during daylight, the landscape took on an otherworldly quality in the night time. Countless eyes glowed around them, their gaze boring into the strangers who trespassed into their realm. He tried to dismiss them as figments of his overstimulated imagination, but the eyes refused to look away.

"I don't understand it," he remarked, trying to distract himself from his fears. "They didn't look like Harappans."

"They weren't," said Shahin. "Don't make the mistake of assuming the Harappans are the only people who have fallen under the spell of Kali. She is an old goddess. Her cult is older than even the gods of your Nubian ancestors, and certainly older than any of the western religions."

"Another reason this cult is so dangerous. People believe that because it is old, it must be true."

"Precisely," Shahin said. "If they aren't drawn to it, they think they cannot resist it because it is something greater than they are. Better to be the right hand of the Destroyer than in her path. At least, that's what they believe."

"Religion is the bane of humanity," Kenda sneered.

His companion did not respond, and he could not tell if Shahin agreed with the assessment. Like most of his personal opinions, the Persian chose to keep this one to himself.

As they continued along the way, Kenda got the distinct impression the eyes weren't only watching them. They were following. With all the predators and venomous creatures about, who needed supernatural foes?

Perhaps his feeling of uneasiness was not merely a false specter conjured up by his imagination?

"Should we keep on the lookout for tigers?" he asked his guide.

"Yes," Shahin said, his voice lowering again. "They like to pounce from behind. I've been watching our backs ever since we lost the thugs. I meant to tell you once you calmed down. Now that you know, you can help me."

"Then we *are* being followed?" He hoped his voice did not squeak.

"Yes," Shahin repeated gravely. "By whom or what, I do not know."

"This just gets better and better..." he groaned.

"Keep moving."

They picked up their pace to a full run.

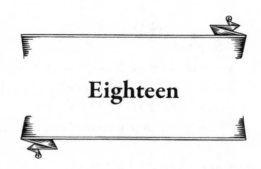

Eighteen

GWENWHYFAR STOOD NEXT to Marcus on the sea shore while they waited for Centurion Brutus to return with the *Varina*.

Etxarte took frequent long walks along the beach, leaving them out of earshot for extended periods of time. She was grateful to him for that. That he left them alone at all demonstrated he at least trusted Marcus as a man of honor. He still made his disapproval clear, but it was a start.

She had no reason to feel anxious when Brutus didn't appear the first day. Patience was a virtue practiced by all who relied upon the sea for travel. A delay didn't always mean a disaster.

"Brutus is an efficient sailor," Marcus assured her. "He'll be here before we know it." He watched her guardian, who exercised among the rocks farther down the shore.

"I don't mind the wait," she said, brushing a strand of hair out of her face. "Tierney will explode like a volcano when he finds out what I've done. Putting that off for a little longer is fine by me. Oh, I don't know what I'm going to tell him! I don't know what I'm going to do."

"Neither do I," he admitted. "But isn't that the beauty of it? Not knowing?"

She looked into his handsome brown eyes.

"Not knowing what kind of future we could have together, I mean," he continued, caressing her cheek. "We're embarking on a beautiful adventure together, just you and me. There is no other person I'd rather make this voyage with."

Etxarte came running toward them. The scarlet sails of the *Varina* rose on the horizon behind him.

"There," Marcus pointed, relieved for a distraction from their dilemma. "What did I tell you?"

WHEN THEY CLIMBED UP on deck from the launch boat, a beaming Brutus stood there to meet them. "Tribune, you're a sight for my old eyes. And you, my lady," he added, with a bow to Gwenwhyfar.

In Marcus' cabin, Brutus gave him some dispatches he'd received. "We're to take them to Sardinia, where another ship will be waiting to receive them. A good thing you were there for me to pick you up, sir. Otherwise, I wouldn't have been able to come back in a long time."

"Luck is on our side," Marcus concurred.

"What of these Vascones? Will they join with us against the Harappans?"

The tribune looked up from the scroll. "Yes, thanks to Lady Gwenwhyfar. Between you and me, I don't know if I could have convinced their leader."

"Fortune does indeed favor us," said Brutus.

It seemed he wished to say more, but chose to keep any further opinions to himself. Marcus detected a mixture of both approval and disapproval from his old friend. The centurion saw much to admire in his young superior's choice in a woman. At the same time, he felt it imprudent on Marcus' part to allow her or any other woman to influence his decisions in the way that she did.

Were Gwenwhyfar any other woman, Marcus might have agreed.

GWENWHYFAR WATCHED the Euskaldunak mountain tops shrink beneath the horizon while she waited for Marcus to finish conferring with his first officer. The sun's diminishing rays shone through the clouds, reflecting off the sea with brilliant streams of color.

Brutus appeared on deck, and gave orders to sail southwest to round Hispania— not what she expected, as Ker-Ys lied to the north.

Marcus joined her soon afterwards to explain. "Before I can return you home, I must deliver some dispatches to Sardinia."

The news thrilled her. It meant that much longer they would spend together. The assignment would take a couple of weeks at a minimum. "Of course you must. I can't tell you how grateful I am to you for everything you've done to help me, tribune."

He grinned, then returned to command his ship.

She watched how the sailors soothed their ship onto her course. Even the rowers seemed willing to play their part. Marcus treated them better than most other captains treated their rowers, even if they were criminals more often than captured prisoners.

Recent events caused the Romans to change their policy regarding the taking of Harappan prisoners, as they did not trust those captives not to call down the elements of sea and sky against them.

All the same, Gwenwhyfar preferred the wind-powered ships of Ker-Ys. They smelled better, for starts.

Leisure and joy filled the next several days. As often as his duties permitted, Marcus spent time with her. Daily they walked the deck together, discussing the future, the classics of philosophy, history, epics, and everything else under the sun.

Far away seemed the war, and all other cares for that matter. Every evening, she and Etxarte dined with Marcus and his officers. It did not take long for the other Romans to come to admire and respect the lady their commander quite obviously adored.

Having caught sight of her from below, the slave rowers improvised songs about her to sing as they kept the oars in rhythm. A part of her felt embarrassed, coupled with her pity for them. Chosen or not, the lot of these men must have surely been a miserable one. She smiled whenever she saw them, careful to leave out any pity in her expression.

Marcus guessed her thoughts. "I once rowed in a galley," he reminded her. "We're not barbarians like the Harappans, or the Carthaginians. Besides, these are criminals. Their judges decided they must repay their debts to Rome."

Etxarte also roamed the decks at his permitted time each day, carrying on his exercises to keep up his strength and keep boredom at bay. He never liked sea voyages, and his disappointment made this one worse.

She felt for him. He wanted the best for her—of that she held no doubt. In his mind, Marcus was not suited for her. She began to wonder if he might ever come around. She didn't want to go against his wishes, and a sorrow filled her heart as a result.

Though he did not understand Latin, Etxarte caught Gwenwhyfar's name in the rowers' chants easily enough. His already raw nerves led him to assume the worst.

He marched over to the command deck right away. "You must put a stop to this!" he demanded. "How dare you allow them to degrade the princess?"

The entire ship heard the accusation.

Marcus, then in the middle of conferring with the centurion and chief navigator, threw down his stylus. "Remember your place on this ship, Breizhian! I would never allow my men to disrespect her. If that did happen, rest assured, they would be severely punished."

Etxarte blinked in confusion.

"They sing of her beauty and virtue," Brutus told him. "They mean to honor her."

A haughty smirk came across Marcus' face. "Ask her yourself if you don't believe me. *She* speaks Latin, after all." He could not help exposing the elder's ignorance. Etxarte's outburst was unacceptable.

Etxarte went below deck without another word.

"I'm sorry for my guardian's rudeness to you," Gwenwhyfar told Marcus later that afternoon. "He means well. I know you must keep order on your ship, but please don't hold it against him. I can't stand against both of you—especially not at once."

He smiled thinly. "I suppose I'd react in the same way. I love you, Gwenwhyfar. That's all I can say. I'd like to offer you a clever line or some dramatic speech, but I can't. I'm a soldier. All I can do is tell you is the truth."

She could all but hear his unspoken thought: *I'm not a learned orator like Petronius.*

"The truth is what I value above all else," she said with adoring eyes. "Where is your confidence, Roman? I've heard you say many clever things."

He risked caressing her hand, in spite of the crew all around them. "I only have trouble believing in myself around you," he whispered. "I could not live with myself if I ever failed you."

"I have confidence that you will not fail me."

AROUND NOON THE NEXT day, the lookout spotted Sardinia.

"Civilization at last," said the centurion. He turned to Etxarte and said in Greek, "I'll show you a real tavern, captain. You'll like it, trust me."

"I look forward to it, along with a decent meal—even Roman cooking is better than weevil-ridden rocks. I intend to fish on the voyage back."

But as they approached the harbor, an uncanny sense of foreboding came over all. Not a soul stood at or near the docks to greet them.

An eerie silence hung on the air. Only the sounds of seagulls and waves splashing against empty boats met their ears.

Etxarte dared to break the stillness. "How many people live here?"

Brutus gulped. "Thousands."

No one worked up the nerve to ask the question foremost on their minds. Marcus did not wait for the men to tie up their ship, but marched forward onto the dock toward town. Gwenwhyfar followed with Brutus and Etxarte.

A ghastly sight awaited them when they reached the first street. They understood now the reason for the silence. The people had not deserted their colony. They were all dead.

Whoever killed them moved through the town with gruesome precision. Merchants and their customers lied on the floor of their shops. In the streets, women clutched their children close to them. Tavern goers lay sprawled over the bar, covered in blood and beer.

Nearly every building bore scorch marks. Fires still burned at every turn. Street stones cracked from the trampling of troops and war chariots. Among the civilians lied the bodies of the legionaries stationed there. They fell while trying to defend their post, and had fought to the last man.

All instinctively drew their swords, as a precaution against any surprises. Marcus ushered Gwenwhyfar to the middle of their group.

"I don't think they even saw the enemy coming," croaked the centurion.

Marcus gripped the hilt of his sword. His knuckled blanched, though his face darkened. "Fan out and search for survivors," he ordered, keeping his tone even.

Outwardly, he displayed a perfect calm. But Gwenwhyfar could see that his mind reeled over the fate of his countrymen. He was scrambling to figure out what to do next. She wanted to throw her arms around his neck and comfort him.

After a giving him a few minutes, she followed, stopping just behind him. She dared not touch him for fear of undermining his authority in front of his crew, or of losing her own control. "You've never seen your people defeated before? Have you?" she choked.

He paused before answering. "Not like this. No."

"Oh, Marcus...I'm sorry," she offered, not knowing what else to say. She found herself unable to banish the thought that this had nearly been the fate of her own beloved Ker-Ys. For all she knew, that fate awaited her city in the future.

The centurion approached. "No survivors yet, sir."

"Keep searching until you've covered the entire town. And don't let your guard down. These fires haven't died. The enemy may still lurk nearby."

Brutus saluted, but didn't leave. The tribune turned back to him.

"You have something to add?"

"Sir, I think they've moved on. The wind blows in an easterly direction. I'd wager my last denarius that's the direction they're headed."

"Yes," agreed Marcus, realization dawning on his features. "They plan to strike Rome herself."

Gwenwhyfar held her hands over her mouth. "Are you certain?"

"Deadly certain, my lady. Because that's exactly what I would do." His jaw hardened. "I'm going to stop them before they get there."

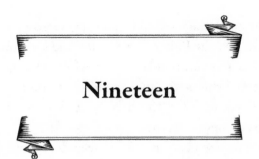

Nineteen

KENDA GRASPED THE SHIP ropes in his hand, savoring the feel of the ocean breeze. They had done it! They escaped India, whole and alive. Shahin managed to book them passage aboard a pirate junk bound for Aksum.

Pirates! Kenda never thought he'd live to see the day he threw his lot in with their kind.

"Smugglers," the Persian had corrected him.

While he did not feel comfortable with their current arrangement, he determined to take things one day at a time. They came this far by that method, and he saw no other way. What a tale to tell his comrades when he returned!

"Where did you dig up this crew?" Kenda demanded, once they were alone. "This is the seediest bunch of cutthroats I've ever seen—almost as bad as those strangler thugs from the jungle!"

"But *not* as bad," said Shahin. "They are all we can afford. More respectable merchants demand more—and they might not take us on to start with."

Their original ship, of course, departed back for Atlantis long before. Kenda imagined the captain waited for them as long as possible, but how could he know their true fate? He surmised King Ashoka sent an apology to Atlantis for the deaths of their representatives, banking on the island continent being in no position to declare war on yet another front.

From Aksum, they would journey across Egypt to the Mediterranean, past the Pillars of Hercules, and southwest to Atlantis. Not as simple as a sail around the tip of Africa, though it would take nearly as long. On this route, they could count on regular commerce and plenty of ports, without worrying about food stores running out as they sailed past endless wilderness.

He would journey near his old homeland. A good thing they did not plan to stop, as he never intended to return there again. Too many terrible memories of his past haunted him. He already saw Jamilia and their children in his dreams often enough.

Shahin suggested they keep watch, taking turns sitting up through the nights. No arguments there. They way this shady crew eyed him—like fresh meat—made his skin crawl.

The food was the worst he'd seen on any ship. Mealy biscuits from the first day out of port. Even when readily available, the purser was too cheap to procure any fruit or vegetables.

"I'll get scurvy before we reach Egypt!" he huffed. "I know it!"

To make matters worse, the cook had strange sores all over his arms and hands. In a vessel this scummy, it did not have surprised him. How did these people function like this?

"She lists to the port," Shahin observed. "One has to wonder how successful these smugglers are, if this is how they maintain their ship."

That made Kenda worry all the more. Come to think of it, they took on their passengers far too eagerly for him to trust their intentions.

"If they pass out sugar cakes," Kenda declared, "I'm jumping overboard."

"I'll be right behind you," he returned.

IT CAME AS NO SURPRISE to them when the captain, a hideous little man with one eye, ordered an attack on the first merchant vessel they encountered.

Kenda and Shahin remained below deck.

"Pray we don't lose this fight," said Shahin. "Otherwise we might find ourselves prisoners again, and awaiting a death sentence on top of that."

"I don't pray," he reminded him. "You're the one who got us into this!"

Shahin returned a wry smile. "What would life be without a little adventure?"

"Safe!" Kenda yelled over the ruckus.

As fortune would have it, they came through the skirmish unscathed. When they dared to venture out of their cabin, they found the crew in the process of dividing up the loot.

The nearest sailor scowled at them. "You didn't fight with us. You don't get a share in the booty."

Shahin held up his hands. "We weren't asking for it. Just checking to see how far we are from Egypt."

"We'll tell you later!" the sailor bellowed. "We're busy right now. Get back below!"

They complied. They could do little else.

"Well, that was interesting," Shahin remarked, when they closed the door of their cabin.

"I'll eat my words now." Kenda laughed. "Am I really hearing this? 'Shahin the Wise and Brilliant' admits he made a mistake? Ha! Maybe there are gods after all."

Shahin didn't share his amusement. "When we arrive at our destination, you can arrange for passage on the next ship, then."

"Gladly," he answered, still reveling in his victory. "*If* we get there, that is." In the meantime, at least he had something else to hold over the Persian.

TO THEIR RELIEF, THE pirates did deliver them to the port of Aksum as promised. Kenda and Shahin got off the cursed boat the instant she docked.

"Somehow," Shahin mused as they made their way across the docks, "I get the feeling we owe our freedom to their...ahem, success."

"I think you're right." Kenda repressed a shudder, not wishing to entertain thoughts of what might have happened otherwise.

The crew jeered at them, as though to confirm Shahin's theory. "Have a good time, pretties," they called.

They did not answer or even look back, but turned their attentions to searching for a place to spend the night. In the morning, they'd think about getting to Egypt.

TWO DAYS DRAGGED ON, and Marcus stared out to sea or paced the decks in anticipation.

The rowers kept the ship moving at a constant speed, pushing at the oars in shifts. In return, he promised them extra rations and a portion of the crew's grog when this was over. An indulgence no other commander would grant them, he was sure.

But he planned for all future scenarios. He might have to call on them to fight for him, as he had during the battle for Ker-Ys. Having earned their freedom, those rowers were gone. He needed to earn the loyalty of these new ones.

He asked Gwenwhyfar and Etxarte to remain below in their cabins for the remainder of the trip. It was wrong to keep his spirited lady cooped up, he knew, but those bewitching amber eyes and silky smooth skin distracted him. To outwit the Harappans and save Rome, he needed his full faculties. Brutus had suggested leaving her and her guardian back at Sardinia, but Marcus could not risk trusting that the Harappans had not left behind any stragglers.

What they encountered at Sardinia was only the beginning. For all he knew, other colonies and outposts had already suffered the same fate.

"That must not happen to Rome," he vowed over and over to himself.

He had not yet formed a complete plan. Only bits and pieces of ideas jumbled around in his head. He still had time before they caught up to the dark ships. They could not have sailed too far ahead. At any moment, the lookout might spy them. He determined to be ready by then.

The other quandary still gnawed at him. What should he do with Gwenwhyfar? She was capable of holding her own, true enough. But he could not give his best in a battle when his head filled with worry about her coming to harm—and this situation demanded the best from him. How could he bear seeing her injured a second time?

He stopped pacing and stared as they sailed past a deserted island. *It won't do to leave her there*, he thought. *She might starve to death if I can't return for her.*

She would not agree to it anyway. That was an understatement—she'd be furious If she shared anything with her elder brother, Tierney, it was a temper. Probably why those two always butted heads, because they were so much alike. He didn't dare suggest that to her, though he pictured how stunning she'd look if he did. Her brilliant eyes would flash at him, her cheeks flushing as she denied the accusation. *She's so beautiful when she loses her temper—*

"Ships ahead!" announced the lookout.

Marcus exhaled. *Just in time.* His imagination had run away with him. He resisted the urge to ask about their identity. The lookout would tell them as soon as he knew himself. He noted Brutus fingering a piece of rope in his hands as they waited.

At last, the lookout had the answer. "Carthaginians!"

A babble of disapproving commentary about their former enemy rumbled over the deck.

"Silence!" Brutus yelled at them.

Marcus felt both frustrated and relieved that they had not caught up to the Harappans. Relief mostly, since he still worked on devising a solution to both his predicaments. "Signal them," he ordered.

Inside of an hour, a Carthaginian officer shouted across the water from the other ship. "Admiral Hamilcar Barca sends his greetings and requests to come aboard for a meeting."

Hamilcar Barca. The man Marcus' father defeated at Mylae. *Well, at least I know who I'm dealing with.*

Barca nurtured a bitter hatred of Rome, Marcus knew. He'd heard that the admiral made his son witness the Roman representatives take away the entire treasury of Carthage after plundering the city. He wanted to ensure that the boy would remember the outrage and one day make Rome pay it all back, with their blood as interest.

For the time being, however, his current loathing of the Harappans superseded the grudges of a past war. A lucky circumstance for Marcus, given who his father was, and that he already met his father's adversary back in Atlantis.

No hope of him not recognizing me. "Signal: Request granted." He turned to Brutus. "Make the necessary preparations. And ask the Lady Gwenwhyfar to come to join us."

The centurion saluted with a knowing twinkle in his eye. "Good idea, sir. She'll have them eating out of her hand, if you'll pardon my boldness."

"Just as I intend them to do."

The Admiral stepped onto the deck of the *Varina* with a dignified poise. He offered a civil nod at the formal introductions.

"Dear lady!" he cried upon seeing Gwenwhyfar. "How did you end up finding yourself at the mercy of these," he caught himself in time, "eh...Romans?"

She flashed a dazzling smile. "Tribune Duilius was gallant enough to rescue me after my ship fell under attack."

"We were en route to returning to Ker-Ys when we learned of enemy ships headed for Rome," Marcus informed him.

Barca nodded, indicating he already knew about the enemy fleet. "Astute of you, bringing her to this meeting to smooth things over."

"Astute, indeed," she said. "Our tribune knows that, as I represent the interests of Ker-Ys, he would incur my displeasure should he not invite me to a conference of allies."

"Naturally, my lady," said Barca with a small bow. "Forgive my arrogant presumption." Already, he was charmed.

They moved to a table of maps to begin their discussion and make plans. Once Barca passed, Marcus gave her a nod of thanks. She responded with a single, raised brow. She meant every word about incurring her displeasure.

What a woman! He forced his back to reality, and focused on the meeting. They discussed and weighed all options they could imagine. In the end, Barca reluctantly agreed to sail with them and come to Rome's aid, if only for the sake of the alliance. Before the next hour passed, they resumed course with the Carthaginian ships to Roman shores.

Marcus couldn't believe this stroke of good fortune. Fifty vessels sailed under Barca's command. With a fleet of that size they had a genuine chance for success. Many in Rome would find offense at Carthage fighting their battles for them—his father might even lead the opposition. But he banished those fears from his mind.

That entanglement can wait for later.

THEY HAD TRAVELED TWO days through the Tyrrhenian Sea when the centurion approached him. "Quartermaster says we've a problem with the water, sir. He requests we stop as soon as possible."

Marcus wanted to scream. All this way, only to be stopped by the water supply? "How many days worth do we have left?"

"It's not so much a matter of levels, tribune."

"What is it, then?" Brutus hesitated. "Better come and have a look for yourself, sir."

The water had spoiled—every single barrel of it. Marcus frowned at the millions of insect larvae squirming around in the container. Were they not on the threshold of battle, he might have had to drink it himself to set an example for the crew.

But Rome lied still four days ahead. Nothing for it, they must stop.

The nearest island was an observation point off Sicily, where a garrison kept an eye on maritime traffic—the traffic from Carthage, particularly, until more recent times. A lighthouse stood on the shore for that purpose.

"The Greeks called it Hiera," he explained to Gwenwhyfar, "but it's hardly considered sacred anymore. Lilybæum lies to the southwest. It takes only a few hours to sail there from here."

Originally a Carthaginian settlement, "the town that looks like Libya" had changed hands multiple times during the war over Sicily. It relieved him they wouldn't go there, as he felt certain Barca would find something to take offense at while in so near proximity to a former colony of Carthage.

Gwenwhyfar shaded her eyes with her hand. "Your family estate lies to the east of the port, doesn't it?"

Marcus swelled with pride. "It does. A pity I can't show it to you. The olives were doing quite well, last I heard."

"Someday you will," she assured him.

"I hope you like it. You may think it's nothing compared to the beauty of Armorica."

"I'm sure I'll love it," she said dreamily. "I look forward to your farmers proudly presenting your fine olives for me to taste."

Seeing her fantasize the event thrilled him all the more. "They will wish to please you more when you're their mistress."

WHAT AWAITED THEM AT the fort proved little different from the carnage at Sardinia.

To their regret, they did not have time to take stock of the damage or search for survivors among the debris. Filling the water barrels as fast as possible, they put back to sea and resumed the chase.

Barca, with his untainted water, had sailed on far ahead.

Marcus watched the Carthaginian sails disappear over the horizon, his frustration mounting. He imagined Barca and his crew laughing and making jokes at their expense. "So much for good luck," he grumbled.

Gwenwhyfar hovered at his side. "I don't think they came near to your home. They're moving too fast to have gone all the way to Sicily. I'm sure your mother and sister are safe."

He turned to look at her exquisite face. If only luck was a lady like her. "They are well...for the moment." He took a moment to steady his voice. "They're in Rome."

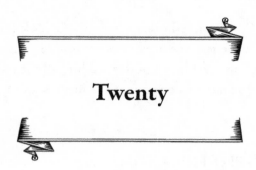

Twenty

HAVING EXHAUSTED ANYTHING and everything he and the Council ever wanted to know about *garum*, plus a whole lot more, Werta croaked through a reading of Plato's *Republic*. Once finished, he intended to follow up with another tangent on the topic of...he'd decide when he reached that point.

"'...And do you see, I said, men passing along the wall carrying all sorts of vessels, and statues and figures of animals made of wood and stone and various materials, which appear over the wall? Some of them are talking, others silent.'"

He had kept at it for over sixteen hours, his voice hoarse, his stomach rumbling, his eyelids heavy, and his legs crossed.

The Council members lounged about in their seats, as miserable as he was, camping out in the Council Chamber all day and half the night, forced to listen while he babbled through this endless rant. But they had the better lot in that they could excuse themselves for a few moments at a time, or doze in their places. Far easier for them to bide their time until the speaker succumbed to the limits of human strength.

"'You have shown me a strange image, and they are strange prisoners.'"

To tell the truth, Werta surprised himself by his endurance. He'd never pursued athletic training or considered himself a prime example of fitness. In school, he was the bookish kid with a soggy belly. The other boys didn't consider him worth challenging to any endurance competitions. Now, he marveled that most of the councilpersons had dozed for periods during his devious tie-up of their plans—and every single one of them had excused themselves more than once.

Not Werta. He outlasted them all.

"'Like ourselves, I replied; and they see only their own shadows, or the shadows of one another, which the fire throws on the opposite wall of the cave...'"

But he would not last for much longer. Early on in the venture, he reveled at the opportunity to tell all the bad jokes people refused to hear under normal circumstances.

Ten hours ago, even he had tired of his own wit. His hoarse voice neared failing completely, while all around him sat a mob desperate to shut him up. His own secretary refused to bring him any more water—not that it would do anything but make things worse by this point.

"'...He will require to grow accustomed to the sight of the upper world. And first he will see the shadows best, next the reflections of men and other objects in the water—'"

A breathless chamberlain threw the doors open. "Begging your pardon, councilpersons, but I carry an urgent message!"

The lethargic Council snapped to attention.

Had a bird flown in, Werta surmised everyone, himself included, would have had a similar reaction—anything to change the monotony of his boring recount of Plato's cave allegory!

"In this case," purred Madam Speaker, "we will make an exception. Deliver your message."

"Ambassador Ptah is alive—here now, and brings important information to be brought before the Council," he exclaimed between breaths. "He begs the Council to postpone their current session while he confers with the Division of Admirals and Generals."

With a weary sigh of surrender, the speaker answered, "Alright. Session adjourned. Go home and get some rest everyone."

To Werta, she added, "You win. This time."

Werta didn't stick around to gloat over her. "Go and tell the Division to start their meeting without me," he blurted to the messenger, "I'll be along in a few minutes."

He stumbled toward the restroom.

AFTER HIS BRIEF DETOUR, Werta arrived at the Division of Admirals and Generals, just down the street from the Council Building.

"It's quite simple," Ptah told them, "their so-called 'magic' is no more than another branch of science. Instead of mechanics powered by water, fire, wind, or the sun, like ours, theirs is based rather upon the energy contained in chemical substances." He stopped, and looked up as the mayor entered.

Werta grinned from ear to ear. "Your arrival is timely, gentlemen. Timely."

"So I've heard," said Ptah. His expression softened. "You look like hell, Nedril."

"You look worse," he chuckled. "If you could see those bags under your eyes. But I've never been happier to see you in all my life." He restrained himself from pulling the two into a bear hug. Common knowledge said a lack of sleep often caused one to succumb to giddiness.

"Tell us more about this technology," said Admiral Itza, getting them back on track.

"Eh, we had to leave sooner than the original plan dictated," Shahin answered. "But I managed to procure a few bits of knowledge here and there. Ashoka seemed open to the idea of exchanging information. At least, he did before we departed without his leave."

"So what are Ashoka's intentions?" asked Werta.

Ptah took over. "As far as we can tell, his claim of a desire for peace is genuine, so long as he doesn't feel threatened. He told us that he once went to war against the Harappans, but failed to defeat them. Then they left India without explanation, vowing to return to fight him again, after they destroyed Atlantis and the lands to the west."

He and Shahin exchanged glances. Werta surmised more went along with that part of story.

"In our opinion," Ptah resumed, "Ashoka will not attack us without provocation. Nor can he sustain an all out war with the Harappans."

Werta held his stare. "Well, there is that. We may not fare any better when it comes to that."

"I think, mayor, that doesn't pose a problem for us," said Itza, weaving his fingers together. "We're more prepared than you think."

Werta raised a brow. "Oh?" This did not bode well.

The admiral hesitated. "There's something I need to show you. I was waiting for the right time. I think this is it." He rose to his feet. "Come with me."

Yawning all the way, Werta followed Itza along with the others to the docks. A small boat ferried them to one of the non-inhabited islands surrounding the continent.

The had long sunk below the horizon, and the light from the boat cast tall shadows on the water ahead of them.

This better be worth it, Werta thought. *I'm about to drop dead.*

After landing in the dark on a thin stretch of beach, they ascended up the path to the jungle interior of the island. Mercifully, they did not travel far before they stopped in front of a gaping cave. A lone guard stood watch at the entrance. He saluted Itza, and stepped aside for the party to pass.

Once inside the massive caverns, Werta was hit with the surprise of his life.

An imposing underground facility stretched out before them. Giant air ships and dirigibles hung above, in the process of construction. Artificial lighting ensured that workers labored through each cycle of the waterclock.

"They're equipped with the latest developments in weaponry and navigation," Itza explained, "including storm-detectors, and a new weapon technology—inspired by electric eels. It's similar to the lighthouse rays, but it uses a different source of power to fire at enemy targets. We began building them just before the siege at Ker-Ys. Unfortunately, none were ready for deployment at that time."

Werta found no words to utter.

"How long has this facility been here?" Shahin ventured.

"My predecessor founded the department. The mainstream powers couldn't be persuaded to see the need for large air ships at that time. The military agreed with them, though now I expect they'll sing a different tune."

Ptah narrowed his eyes at the admiral, but allowed for him to finish.

"Our false sense of security has prevailed for too long," Itza continued. "We took the initiative and began testing the prototypes our own."

Werta rubbed his burning eyes. "Wait...just wait. Why wasn't I told about any of this?"

"Two words, mayor: plausible deniability." The admiral held his hands behind his back. "If information ever leaked out to the public, answers would be demanded from you. You in turn would deny it, and the people would believe you."

"Because I would believe it myself." He groaned.

Itza replied with a nonchalant shrug. "When the time came, the people and politicians would be angry. At first. But they'll thank us in the end."

"So where did the funding for all of this come?" asked Ptah, barely concealing his chagrin.

Itza faced him. "No one ever told me, and I didn't ask."

Anger boiled in Werta's blood. "When this war is over, I'm going to fire you."

Itza looked back with a stoic expression. "I imagined you would say that when you learned of this."

"Yes, yes. I know. You'll be considered a hero, at which point I *can't* fire you."

"Such is the lot of great military leaders. I will indeed be a hero." Itza held his head high and proud. "Because I took the steps necessary to protect Atlantis."

"At what cost?" Werta shouted. "The cost of us sliding down the slope to becoming no different from our enemy, that's what! Accepting that the ends of victory justify the means of deceiving and stealing from the people."

Ptah backed him up. "He's right. The next thing we know, we've thrown away all we've accomplished as a civilization and degenerated back to sacrificing bulls, followed by our children—mark my words—upon the altars of insatiable deities!"

"You're overreacting, captain," the admiral responded.

"Are we?" Werta asked. "Hasn't Atlantis learned by now? History shows this is how it always starts."

"Atlantis will survive because of what I've done!" Immediately after the outburst, Itza composed himself, though his tawny cheeks still flushed. "You, too, will thank me eventually. Fatigue has clouded your judgment, mayor."

Werta shook his head. He felt too tired to give Itza the dressing down he deserved. "Tell yourself that, if it helps you sleep at night. Personally, I won't have any trouble. For now, I'll bid you all goodnight. We'll discuss this further in the morning."

The others made way as he made for the exit.

His way home passed in an unmemorable blur. The dark sky began to lighten. Morning had come.

He didn't bother to change his clothes when he at last stepped over the threshold of his home. He lost consciousness the instant his head hit the pillow.

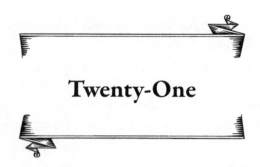

Twenty-One

AT HIGH NOON, THE *Varina* sailed in close enough to view the port of Ostia.

The Harappan attack had already broken out into a chaotic fray. Fire flew from one vessel to another. Several ships lay on their sides, sinking. Gwenwhyfar noted that most of those belonged to Rome or Carthage. The *Varina* sailed on through the flotsam and jetsam toward the port.

Boom! The dark ships shot strange, round projectiles, which exploded upon impact with their targets.

Gwenwhyfar took in the scene around her. *The gods help us!*

The precision of those weapons impressed her as nearly on par with Atlantis' lighthouse rays, though not nearly as far-reaching. It seemed that at every encounter the Harappans brought forth some never before seen weapon. Would they ever run out of new armaments?

She clenched her fists, and moved to draw her sword from its sheath. *Let them bring on their tricks! Just wait until we get close enough.*

Marcus stopped her, gently putting his hand over hers.

"You don't want me on board when you attack," she said, speaking his thoughts aloud. "But you need every available person who can wield a sword. And don't try to convince me otherwise. I'm not naïve, Marcus."

His lips thinned into a firm line. "You speak the truth. I don't want you to fight. I admit it. I can't forget the time I found you on that battlefield. I thought you were dead, and I didn't know how I was going to live."

She exhaled sharply, knowing that at any time now, Etxarte would soon join them with his own arguments why she shouldn't come with them. How could she stand against both of them together?

"But my feelings aren't why I'm asking you not to fight." He pointed toward Ostia. "The enemy has already landed. Even now, they're on the way to sack Rome." He took both her hands into his. "Gwenwhyfar, please, I need you to find my mother and sister. I can't leave my ship to rescue them. Get them out of there."

Anger rose to her cheeks. Did he expect her to swallow that excuse?

He grasped her by the shoulders. "They have courage, but they can't fight like you can. You're strong and capable and beautiful! I know you can save them and take them home to Sicily!"

She couldn't bare to hold his desperate gaze. "You're wrong, Marcus. I'm not brave. If I were brave, I'd let you face this engagement by yourself. War is the path you've chosen, the path you always claim will lead you to glory. But I'm a coward. I cannot give you the glory of having won your battles alone. I'm afraid to lose you."

"We'll meet again in Sicily," he insisted, calming himself. "Don't you see? The danger to those in Rome won't end when the battle is over. The chaos will continue. Looters and stragglers will plunder the city. Food will run out."

That hadn't occurred to her. It hadn't happened in Ker-Ys. But then again, she didn't witness the immediate aftermath of the siege. She vaguely recalled the reports of chasing off the stragglers, but that was all. The enemy armada in front of them here was decidedly larger.

Rome was different from Ker-Ys. It was a sprawling metropolis, dotted by shady areas where shady types roamed. Both Petronius and Finn had warned her never to visit such places. A disaster would provide the perfect chance for those opportunists to try their luck and for once evade the authorities.

The aftermath would prove a nightmare for the residents of Rome. Marcus was not spinning a ploy to keep her safe. His mother and sister truly were in danger.

"You're the only person I can ask to do this without fear of dishonor," he said. "If you love me, you must do this for me."

He was right again, she realized. To send one of his men away from the battle was impossible. Honor would demand the unfortunate soldier fall on his sword afterwards—or risk disgrace to his own family's good name. She was the only one who could help the man she loved.

She searched his handsome brown eyes. "You don't think you'll survive, do you? If you love me, don't lie to me."

He swallowed. "I don't know. Probably not," he admitted. "But I will fight all the harder if I know the women I love most in the world are safe. Can you not look on my family as your own?"

Tears stung her eyes. "Yes, I'll do this for you, my love. I'll do anything for you!"

"Then let me take the memory of your kiss into battle with me." He held her in his strong arms and kissed her with all the passion of his being, no longer caring if his crew saw them.

The sounds and sights around them faded, and she felt aware of only Marcus, the man she loved more than life itself.

AGONY WRENCHED GWENWHYFAR's heart as the crew lowered her and Etxarte down from the trireme deck and into the tiny boat bobbing on the water below. She might never see her gallant tribune again. Tears filled her eyes, but she held them back, refusing to permit them to rob her of her last memory of him.

Etxarte loosed the line and tossed it up to the waiting hands on deck.

"I love you!" she called.

"I know," Marcus answered. "*Vale, carissime.*"

The moment they floated clear of the oars, Marcus gave the command for battle speed. Within the bowels of the *Varina*, a drummer pounded the rapid pace. Grunting rowers plowed the waves, propelling their ship and her tribune far away within minutes.

The tears she had held back began to fall without restraint.

"It's for the best," Etxarte said behind her, paddling his way toward the shore. "He's not suited for you."

His words wore down the last remnants of her control. "You don't understand," she said between sobs. "I love him! We can't always choose...who we fall...in love with! You'd know that...if you...had a heart!"

Etxarte nearly dropped the paddle over the side as he took her into his arms. "My poor child! You think I don't have a heart? Don't you understand how much I love you?"

She sobbed harder.

"Why can't you see he's not good enough for you? The Romans think they own the world—oh, hell!" His voice broke. "We'll find the women and bring them to his home. When he comes back, I'll find some way to convince your brothers to let you marry him. I don't know how, but I will. Please don't cry, my girl!"

She sniffed, looking up into his sad, gray eyes. "You mean that?"

He stroked her hair. "Yes, I mean it. I still say he doesn't deserve you. But if you made up your mind that you must have him—curse this sea water, it's burning my eyes."

He held her close and let her cry into his chest. "If he hurts you, I'll bash his brains out."

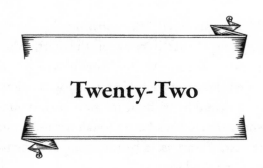

Twenty-Two

IF ONLY GWENWHYFAR had listened to her instincts. She knew they should have taken the left instead of the right back there. They would have to loop around the *insulae*.

Not that she objected to their making use of an abandoned chariot. What she did regret was that she'd allowed her memories of Rome to drift away, as one did when trying to forget a nightmare. Along with her painful past went the knowledge of the city's layout. The gathering darkness made their surroundings take on an unfamiliar air.

"Romans drive on the left side," she instructed Etxarte.

"It's not like it matters," he objected, skirting a yelping dog in his path. "No one else is following the rules in this madhouse! Everyone's trying to get out—we're the only fools trying to get in!"

Rome indeed lay in a state of chaos. Between the Harappan soldiers, native vacillators, and panicking plebeians, the streets overflowed with running, screaming people.

Etxarte, not having visited a large city previously, much less one besieged, found himself continuously flabbergasted at the frenzy. "How does this city function? We're like a fish swimming upstream!"

Her guardian had always wanted to drive a chariot, so he insisting on taking the reins. He'd done well for his first time, considering the circumstances. Gwenwhyfar stood at his side, holding on for dear life.

Under any other circumstances, she would have worried about returning to the place where her life took a turn for the worst. Rome was where she experienced her first taste of corruption and violence.

Terrible though this visit was, at least she didn't have to worry about Petronius' and Scipio's families wreaking vengeance upon her for a crime she did not commit.

Focus on the task at hand, she reminded herself.

"Maniac!" shrilled a woman on the sidewalk. She'd barely managed to pull her child to safety before they blew past them.

"Next time don't walk your brat in the middle of the street!" Etxarte yelled back.

"Lookout!" Gwenwhyfar cried.

He turned his attention forward just in time to veer around a driver coming from the opposite direction.

The horses reared to a screeching halt, nearly throwing Gwenwhyfar from the vehicle.

A centurion competed for the right of way. His wife and daughter clung to either side of him. "Dumb ox!" he yelled. "Drive on the right side of the road!"

Etxarte couldn't understand his words, but he took his meaning well enough. He responded with his own string of insults.

Gwenwhyfar stepped out and stood between them. "Please, centurion," she entreated, "can you tell us the way to the house of Duilius?"

Given the fame achieved by Marcus' father, she held every confidence this soldier knew.

Upon seeing a woman in his path, his chagrin faded. "Two blocks that way," he pointed. "Fifth house, on the north side of the street."

Had Etxarte been the one to step in front of him, she suspected the officer might have ran right over him without the slightest hesitation. He guided his horses around her to speed off toward Ostia.

"Thank you!" she called after him.

They pushed on deeper into the city, toward the conflagration and screams. Soon they encountered more pillaging Harappan soldiers. Gwenwhyfar drew her sword. While Etxarte mowed several down under their wheels, she dispatched any others in range with Euskaldunak steel.

"You're aiming too low," her teacher critiqued. "There's no excuse for sloppy strokes at any time!"

They nearly passed the place.

He pulled back on the reins to stop. The front door hung on a single hinge, broken through. It creaked with the blowing wind. Inside, the flickering of moving candles indicated there were still people within the villa's walls.

"Don't come any closer," came a woman's frightened voice from inside.

Weapons ready, they crept up the stairs and peered through the opening. His bow drawn, Etxarte kicked the door off its hinge.

Three enemy soldiers cornered the two women—Marcus' mother and sister!

With the element of surprise on their side, they quickly felled the Harappans. She and Etxarte lowered their weapons.

"Any more of them in the house?" Gwenwhyfar asked them in Latin.

The women shook their heads, still in a state of fright.

"I am Princess Gwenwhyfar Meur of Ker-Ys," she introduced herself, "and this is my guardian and Captain of the Guard, Heranal Etxarte. Tribune Duilius sent us here to rescue you."

She had imagined this moment many times, but her potential mother and sister-in-law looked quite different from the mental image she'd formed. They dressed the part of patricians, to the extent Gwenwhyfar might never have believed otherwise if she did not already know of their more humble origins.

Marcus may have taken more after his father, but she still saw a family resemblance. Both women had the same light brown hair, the same catching brown eyes.

Lady Æliana recovered from her shock and drew herself up. "Why should we believe you? A couple of barbarians burst into our home, and you expect us to trust you?"

"Mother!" entreated Gaia. "They just saved our lives!"

She's not much younger than I, Gwenwhyfar realized. She knew Roman matrons were infamous for their haughtiness. All the same, she could not let the insult slide.

"Barbarians! Our people claimed land from the sea while you Romans still lived in mud huts!"

Etxarte grasped her arm. "We don't have time for this. We must leave before more of them return."

She calmed herself. "Lady Duilius, don't you think you're better off coming with us than taking your chances with *those* barbarians?"

"She's right, mother," agreed Gaia.

But Æliana still harbored suspicion. "Just where is it you want us to go?"

"Tribune Duilius wishes us to bring you to your estate in Sicily," she answered. "He will meet us there after the battle."

"Leave the safety of Rome?" she scoffed. "I can hardly believe my son would ask that."

"He would if we were no longer safe in Rome," urged Gaia. "The legions here cannot protect us. Marcus sent her because he must stay with his ship. Listen to reason, mother."

A loud crash sounded from the rear of the house.

"We're leaving," commanded Etxarte. "Now."

"BEAT TO QUARTERS!" Marcus ordered "Drummers: Battle speed!"

The Harappan armada turned from the port and headed right for them. His Roman soldiers stood ready at their battle stations. Beneath his feet, he felt the rumble of the drummers pounding out the rhythm for their rowers' timing chant.

All eyes on deck rested on the *Varina's* commander. Within minutes, they would plunge themselves into absolute chaos.

In his anticipation, Marcus instinctively tensed the muscles in his back. "They're men just like us," he reminded the marines. "They bleed and die like us, too."

At his side, the centurion leaned near his ear. "Whether we live or die, sir, I have faith you'll save Rome."

"Thank you, Brutus," he acknowledged. "I hope your faith in me will not prove in vain."

"It is an honor to serve with you, tribune, as it was my honor to serve with Gaius."

Marcus smiled. "Likewise, centurion. I am grateful for your wisdom and guidance. They have been invaluable to me."

He bowed his head. "The admiral is proud of you, sir. He told me so."

The tribune tightened his jaw to hold back the rush of emotion he felt. He would have preferred to have heard those words from Gaius himself, yet it meant a great deal to hear them all the same.

Brutus changed the subject. "Ironic. In all my years of service, I never thought I'd live to see the day we fought with Carthage instead of against her."

"The gods have a sense of humor," the younger agreed with a wry grimace.

"That they do, tribune."

Balls of fire now flew through the air toward them. The expected waterspouts formed next, churning up the sea into a boil. At the urging of their sorceresses, the Harappan fleet chanted themselves into a fury. The rage of fanaticism consumed them.

The centurion held his hand up, preparing to issue the first orders of the engagement. "Basilisks: ready!" he reported.

"Fire!" Marcus yelled. "For Rome!"

Brutus took up the battle cry. The marines followed his lead. "Rome!"

All hell unleashed.

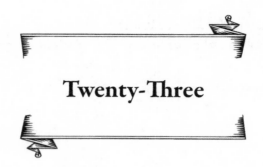

Twenty-Three

ETXARTE HURRIED HIS three charges into the chariot. He looked around. "A good thing all of you are women. Four men can't fit in this thing."

Another crash from inside urged him to get going. The Harappan warriors burst out onto the street right as they hurried off.

Gwenwhyfar exhaled. Even with the chariot weighted down, they traveled too fast for their enemy to pursue on foot. She consoled herself with the knowledge that looters preferred easy targets.

"Going back to the harbor's no good," Etxarte observed. "That way would be like trying to push through a feeding frenzy of sharks."

Gwenwhyfar had not considered that. She asked Gaia's opinion, careful to avoid the disparaging gaze of Æliana.

"We should exit the city and go south," the girl suggested. "We can leave by another port"

The princess searched her memory. "Near Capua?"

"Yes," said Gaia. "Take the Via Appia. Go right at this next intersection."

Gwenwhyfar translated for Etxarte.

"South it is, then," he agreed.

Making the turn on one wheel, he drove right through a flock of chickens that appeared around the corner. The birds squawked and flew in all directions, sending feathers flying everywhere. "This is insane!" he yelled.

Ahead of the chickens loomed a mob of frightened people. "Look!" a man from the crowd shouted. "Horses! A chariot!"

The horde rushed toward them.

Etxarte wrapped the reins about his fists. "Hold on," he warned. "Don't let them overpower us, no matter what." He charged forward into the crowd.

Gwenwhyfar flinched with the sudden lurch, but held her sword ready.

The mob engulfed them. Æliana and Gaia screamed, but managed to hold on. Their veils were ripped away, their dresses torn. But they didn't let go of the chariot.

Gwenwhyfar made use of her sword's hilt, trying not to resort to the sharp edge of her blade. But she knew she'd cut down a few.

Etxarte alternated between whipping the horses and their attackers. He never stopped moving.

They had nearly made it through when someone yanked Gwenwhyfar's long braid, pulling her into the swarm. She hit the hard stones of the street, her breath taken away. People ran over her.

The chaos around her blurred. She gasped for air like a fish out of water. If she didn't get up soon, the people would trample her to death.

By some miracle, two arms dragged her out from under the mob's footsteps. She never caught sight of her rescuer, though she afterwards recalled hearing a brief, "Be well," before the man hurried off.

When she caught her breath and her vision cleared, she found herself leaning between the posts of a doorway. To her relief, her fist still gripped her sword. She pushed herself to her feet.

Further down the street, Etxarte and the women looked all around for her, their faces filled with horror.

"Meet me around the corner!" she cried out to them.

But the sea of humanity drowned out her voice. Her companions continued to search for her, but were soon pushed farther away from her by the masses. They had no choice but to move on. Etxarte was clearly heartbroken.

Gwenwhyfar's own heart wrenched in sadness for him. *I'll catch up to you*, she promised.

She kept to the side of the building, and pulled herself into what she discovered was a local pub. The bartender had fled long before along with his customers, save a lone drunkard.

"You're beautiful!" He raised his mug to her, downed it, then staggered to the public restroom next door—as though the sacking of Rome was just another day.

If one believed he was going to die anyway, why not? She shrugged. *At least he made it to the privy.*

After all she had witnessed that day, nothing struck her as odd any more. Rubbing her temples, she collected her thoughts.

Via Appia... The road lied just to the west, didn't it? She tried once more to recall the city's layout, regretting that she expended so much effort into forgetting everything to do with her former home, never imagining she might need those memories again.

"West," she decided.

Not that she remembered, but that it seemed logical. With luck, she'd meet up with Etxarte and the others just outside of the city, if not before. Her guardian would get Marcus' mother and sister to safety, of that she felt certain.

No matter what happened, she intended to press on until she reached Sicily. "I must get there. I must see Marcus again." She repressed the slew of fears that threatened to raise their ugly heads, and pushed her way through the streets.

The crowd had thinned somewhat, and the people around her were either fleeing themselves, or too busy taking advantage of the situation. A handful of Roman soldiers arrived on the scene to put out fires and fight off the looters.

After a while, she became aware of a pair of eyes on her. She scanned the streets, but everyone seemed too caught up in their own difficulties to notice her. She tried to dismiss the notion, yet it returned again and again.

Someone dogged her steps. But who, and why?

As far as she saw, no one seemed to take interest in her amidst the anarchy and disorder. All the same, she heeded her instincts, subtly glancing over her shoulder every so often. Goosebumps prickled on her arms.

Then she spotted him—a Harappan warrior.

He ducked into doorways or behind overturned carts to avoid her searching glance. *One of the leaders*, she surmised, if her memory of their insignia served.

Hairs rose on the back of her neck, and she shuddered in spite of the heat from the fires. Something about him felt eerily familiar, like a specter from a forgotten nightmare. Smiley instantly came to mind.

No, he's dead, she reminded herself. *I took his head myself.* This one didn't match Smiley's stature anyway. A reason she associated her stalker with Finn's killer existed. But she could not place how or why.

The next thing she noticed was that he never overtook her, though by then he'd had ample opportunity. She could not catch a second look at him. By now, that section of the street was devoid of people. Off in the distance, she still heard the sounds of a city besieged.

Cold sweat trickled down her temples. She felt trapped, like in a nightmare, trying to escape an unseen hunter. At any moment, she might become his prey.

She took a deep, calming breath. *This isn't a dream. I have complete control over my circumstances.*

Curiosity soon replaced fear, until she determined to discover the identity of this mysterious stranger. While he hid himself from her gaze, she slipped underneath an abandoned cart. A torn grain sack hanging over the side obscured her from sight. There, she waited.

Sure enough, his sinewy, tawny legs appeared in the street. His upper body remained out of her line of vision, and she did not dare expose herself for the sake of a better look. One thing was without question: he *was* seeking her.

She held her breath in her throat. She had given him the slip. For now.

He pored over the area, knowing she could not have gotten far without his discovering which way she went. She didn't have much time before he found her.

She held her sword ready. *You will meet the same fate as your comrade*, she vowed. She'd attempt to guess his identity from his fallen corpse at her feet. Right now, she must focus on defending herself.

Having completed his sweep of one side of the street, he loomed closer to her hiding spot.

She poised to strike. *I'll stab his leg*. That way, if she did not manage to kill him, at least she might escape.

A Roman horn sounded. More auxiliaries arrived.

He turned and fled, just as the Romans rounded the corner. The soldiers marched past her, heading toward Ostia.

Relieved, she slipped out from under the cart. The Harappan was nowhere to be found.

Rejoicing in her newfound stroke of luck, she dashed off to meet up with her companions.

THE CITY OF ROME ROARED in flames.

Gwenwhyfar felt relieved that Ker-Ys had been spared this experience. Only now did she fully grasp Marcus' concern about his mother and sister. If she and Etxarte hadn't come for them, they might have perished in this madness.

A sea of people surrounded her, all clamoring for relief from their suffering. She had to get back off the street. But then what? *Then...I'll decide what to do when I get there.*

Pushing through the hoard of humanity, she made for a nearby alley. People tore at her hair and clothes. The crowd pulsed with insane fear.

The way through seemed impossible. Panic threatened to seize her and carry her off with everyone else. Her hand moved to the hilt of her sword. Reason stopped her. Cutting people down wouldn't solve her problem.

"Let me through!" she cried. Her voice was lost in the noise.

A large fountain stood in the corner of the square. Making it there wouldn't get her out of the city, but it would give her a few moments' respite. There, she could at least plan her next move.

She shoved through the people and made for the fountain, nearly stepping on a young girl, who had fallen to the ground. Caught in the moment, it was tempting to leave the child behind. But then she remembered the man who helped her earlier.

Pulling the child into her arms, she pressed on toward the fountain. "Hold on," she said, uncertain if the girl even heard her. "Almost there."

She intended to sit on the wide rim, but instead they were shoved into the chilly water. The pool wasn't deep however, and she found she felt safer in the water away from the violence than on the ledge. The girl shivered.

Inside the pool, a statue of a nymph riding a fish sprayed water toward the center sculpture. She lifted the girl onto the statue. "Today's your lucky day," she said. "You get to ride a fish with this nymph. How many other children are allowed to play in the fountains?"

"Are you sure father won't scold me?" she asked, her eyes wide.

"I know he'll understand for tonight." Those words calmed the child. "Just sit there for a moment while I think."

Gwenwhyfar leaned against the fish statue and folded her arms around her body for warmth. For a several minutes, she simply stood there, watching in disbelief at the mighty city of Rome in flames. The sight filled her with sorrow. "Oh, Marcus, I'm glad you aren't here to see this!"

Miles away on the sea, he struggled in his own battle. She wondered how he fared, and couldn't help but worry if she'd ever see him again.

"Who is Marcus?" the girl asked.

"Rome's greatest hero," she answered. "As we speak, he fights on the sea to keep more of those evil men from coming ashore here. Tribune Marcus Duilius—always remember his name, child."

"I will," the girl promised. "Are you going to marry Tribune Duilius?"

Gwenwhyfar smiled, her heart lightened for the first time in what felt like an age. "I hope so."

"Is he handsome?" Her little round face leaned forward.

"Very handsome."

"Then you should marry him," said the girl, as though that settled the matter.

Gwenwhyfar laughed. Of course, she must help the child. How could she hope to find her family on her own?

As though in answer to her unspoken question, she caught sight of a man driving a cart at the edge of the crowd. In the cart with him sat a woman and a small boy. Instinct told her they must be the little girl's family.

The man likewise saw Gwenwhyfar and the girl, since they were the only ones standing in the fountain. He looked about for a way through to them.

"Mama!" the girl cried.

"We'll get to them," Gwenwhyfar assured her.

Her eye traveled to the awnings above the store fronts along the street. If she could reach one of those, they might make their way to where the family in the cart waited. But would the awnings hold their weight?

Risking a pivot on the ledge nearest the first awning, she tossed the girl up. "Stay there and wait for me!" she called.

The girl held still.

Gwenwhyfar leaped to catch the bar of the canopy, thanking the gods it did not give way and drop her and the girl onto the ground below. *Romans know how to build*, she marveled. *I'll never speak ill of them again.*

She threw her right foot over the top, but nearly lost her grip when a looter caught her other leg. "Where are you going, barbarian wench?" He uttered an evil laugh. "Down to me! I'll show you Roman hospitality."

It was the girl who came to her rescue. Procuring a pole from the upper sunshade, she bashed the assaulter on the head. He fell to the ground and disappeared beneath the feet of the crowd.

Gwenwhyfar rolled into the awning. "Thank you, child," she returned between breaths.

Bad enough for enemy Harappans to sack the city, but citizens turning on their own people? Her opinion of Roman justice changed then and there. That scoundrel deserved to row in the galleys.

She got to her knees, and pointed to the next overhang. "That way."

They jumped from awning to awning around the perimeter of the forum. They well-nigh fell through one that had ripped, but otherwise made it around without incident. At the last overhang, they saw the remaining distance was too wide for them to jump across.

The rooftop. She caught the father's eye again, and pointed to the roof. They must meet on the other side.

He nodded, and steered his donkey in that direction.

Lifting the girl to the roof, she pulled herself up. They made they way past hanging herbs left out to dry, along with dozens of *amphorae* filled with olives, *garum*, and wine.

The family already waited there when they slipped down the other side.

"Oh, thank you! Thank you!" the mother cried, taking her girl into her arms.

"May the gods reward you for your kindness," said the father. "We have room for you if you'd like to come along."

"Are you going south?"

"Yes. Come with us. It's the least we can do for you." He helped her into the cart.

They journeyed down the Via Appia with many more refugees. Long after the city disappeared from sight, a massive column of smoke could still be seen, coupled with the terrible glow of conflagration.

Gwenwhyfar and the wife glanced back every so often, still in disbelief at what had become of mighty Rome.

The man kept his eyes forward and drove their donkey, his face an emotionless mask. "You will rebuild," she told the wife.

"My home has survived an attack by the Harappans, and we have made a new start. We are not so powerful as Rome, and we've survived. You will, too."

The sun set, but the flicker of fire lit their way down the road for many hours. Ahead, Gwenwhyfar caught sight of a chariot. Two Roman women stooped in exhaustion on either side of a man in the black garb of a Breizhian captain.

"Etxarte!" she cried, leaping out of the cart. She turned to the family. "Thank you for your help!"

When he saw her, Etxarte's weary face filled with joy and relief. "My girl!" He pulled on the reigns to stop the horse.

She rushed into her guardian's arms. He held her close, and she felt his beard prickling into her forehead.

"I thought I had surely lost you," he said, exchanging waves of gratitude with the man in the cart.

They stepped into the chariot. "Good to have you back. These two women are impossible to talk to," he added with a wink.

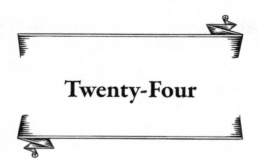

Twenty-Four

TRAVELING SOUTH PROVED little easier than trying to return to Ostia. Chaos reigned unchallenged down the Via Appia out of the city as desperate Roman citizens tried to escape their burning city.

Many at first brought their possessions with them, only to leave them abandoned on the side of the road. The resulting bottleneck slowed their exodus all the more.

Long into the night they traveled through the countryside. The crowd gradually thinned out, as people took differing forks along the road. Etxarte continued to drive them south.

"We must stop," Æliana urged, rubbing her shoulders. "I can go no longer. It's so cold."

"Yes, please tell your captain," said Gaia. "I'm too weary to stand anymore."

Gwenwhyfar had entertained those same thoughts herself. "A few hours of sleep would do us *all* good," she said, placing a hand on her guardian's shoulder.

Etxarte stopped the chariot. He might have gone all night and the following day, if the situation called for it. But the look of relief on his face showed his relief it did not call for it.

"There's a barn up ahead." He pointed to the structure at the top of the hill. "Let's pray it's abandoned. I don't think the farmer will let us sleep there if he knows."

They drove up the winding path to the barn. It wasn't abandoned. Horses and cows stood sleeping in the stalls. The animals stirred when the door opened.

Etxarte shot a cautious glance at the farm house down the way, hoping the owners hadn't heard their horses startled neighs. A dog barked off in the distance.

"Sons of the *morghens*," he cursed.

"Let's just talk to them," Gwenwhyfar suggested. "Asking will cost us nothing." She glanced toward Æliana and Gaia. "I think the farmer may respond more favorably if a Roman lady asked him."

Æliana shook her head, and collapsed to her knees in weariness.

"I'll ask," said Gaia.

The barking dog bounded down the path toward them, his angry master close behind. "Who are you? How dare you trespass on my property?" He waved his pitchfork at them in warning.

"Please, sir," said Gaia, holding up her hands in defense. "I am Lady Gaia Duilius, daughter of Admiral Duilius. This is my mother, and our two friends, the princess of Ker-Ys and her guard. We are fleeing Rome to safety—"

"You and everyone else!" he interrupted. "I've fought off you refugees from Rome all day!"

"We ask you only to sleep in your barn tonight," she persisted. "And perhaps, something for our horse?" Her voice faltered. "We have no where else to turn. Our family is wealthy. Tell us your name and my father will repay you many times over as soon as we are able."

"Duilius?" He scratched the back of his head. "Yes, I know that name." His hands fell to his sides. "If I help you, every other refugee pouring out of Rome will invade my home."

"We have no where else to turn..." she repeated.

"Oh, alright," he resigned. "But you'd better not steal any of my livestock, or I'll take my case all the way to the Senate. I may not be a patrician, but I have rights as a citizen!"

It was a hollow threat, given that Gaius held the position of consul, but he was desperate to protect his livelihood.

"We will respect your property," Gaia assured him.

Again, the farmer scratched the back of his head. "You can have some of the hay for your horse," he grumbled. "And...I suppose I can send you something to eat, my lady."

"Thank you," said Gaia. "My father will reward you. You have my word."

He waved her away and made for his house, commanding his dog to his heel.

"Well done," said Gwenwhyfar. Gaia smiled in return.

"There's only one entrance," Etxarte observed. "You women sleep in the loft, and I'll lay by the door. We can't assume we're completely out of danger."

Gwenwhyfar agreed, and translated for the others.

Æliana considered their accommodations beneath her dignity. She did not complain, however, but pulled herself up the ladder. Gwenwhyfar and Gaia followed her.

While her mother fell asleep by herself in one corner, Gaia settled into a cozy pile of hay near Gwenwhyfar. "I always wanted to sleep in a pile of hay when I was a girl," she whispered. "Just like the stable hands."

Gwenwhyfar chuckled quietly. "I can't say I've shared your wish. I wanted to sleep in the forest beneath the trees in summertime."

"Weren't you worried about wild animals?" Gaia asked with wide eyes.

"Well, yes. That's why I never did it." Her cheeks warmed. Gaia had such brilliant eyes—eyes that indicated intelligence and wisdom beyond her years. *Just like her brother's eyes.*

On the floor below, Etxarte tended to their horse. He liked horses, and had a special way with them. He gave the animal a generous pile of hay and stroked his coat, speaking to him in a kind, soothing voice.

Gwenwhyfar considered the poor creature must have suffered the same trauma as they had.

She turned her gaze back over to the sleeping Æliana. It was obvious the matron did not approve of her. Marcus would be disappointed when he found out. Or maybe he already knew? She exhaled and rolled over onto her back.

"She's trying her best," said Gaia. "We are not accustomed to these hardships, but we'll manage."

"I don't blame her," said Gwenwhyfar. "This isn't to my liking, either."

"Marcus loves you dearly, you know," said the girl. "I'm happy to know you care for him, too. It would crush him if you didn't. Do not let our mother persuade you to give him up. She will relent eventually."

Gwenwhyfar was taken aback. "Is it obvious that I love him?"

Gaia smiled. "You wouldn't have saved our lives at risk to your own if you didn't love him. I'll be happy to have a princess for a sister."

She frowned. "Even if that princess is a barbarian?"

Gaia laughed. "Barbarian, indeed! You are everything my brother said. Did you not tell mother yourself that your civilization is older than even our fair city—" She stopped herself as the memory of Rome in trouble returned.

"Marcus will succeed," said the princess. "Rome will have troubles for a while, but he will right them. After he's done that, he'll come back to us."

"Yes, you are right." She wiped away her welling tears and composed herself. "I must remain strong for mother. But you're so brave, Lady Gwenwhyfar. I wish I had your courage."

Marcus' words flooded back to her. *Gaia and mother have courage, but they can't fight like you can.* "You have more courage than you know," she told her. "I, too, will be pleased to have you for a sister."

"I'm glad you think so. Goodnight." Gaia closed her eyes, and drifted off to sleep.

Before she knew it, Gwenwhyfar likewise succumbed to exhaustion.

THEY SET OFF AT THE break of dawn.

"Better make for the port of Capua," the farmer advised. "It's farther away, but you'll have a better chance of finding a ship there to take you to Sicily." He begrudgingly handed them a bag of cheese and brined olives, and a skin of wine. "My wife sends this. It's all we can spare."

Gaia thanked him, and once more promised to repay him in the near future.

They made their way through the lovely countryside, past hills of grapes and olives, past fields of emerging wheat, and green pastures blooming with spring flowers. Cows lowed at them every so often from the side of the road.

The horrors of war seemed far away, like some distant memory. None of them dared to allow the fantasy to seduce them.

"To think what will happen to all of this if they didn't win the battle..." Æliana uttered.

"Your son is one of Rome's finest commanders," said Gwenwhyfar. "If anyone can defeat the enemy armada, it is he. Remember, he saved my city once before. Think how much harder he will fight for his own people."

CAPUA CROWDED WITH refugees, who continued to pour into the coastal city. It held no candle to what they witnessed in Rome, however. After that experience, this town felt to Gwenwhyfar as no more hectic than market day in Ker-Ys.

Etxarte stopped the chariot at an empty spot near the wharf. "Wait here. I'll go arrange for passage on one of these ships."

While he was gone, Gaia addressed one of the dock hands. "Tell me, sir, is there any news of the battle?"

"Certainly over by now, my lady," he said, "though no word has reached us yet." He shook his head. "The bodies of those poor souls are already washing ashore."

Two other men carried one of the washed up corpses to a cart for burial. "We're waiting either for a messenger," said one of them, "or the invasion fleet to strike us."

Gaia and Æliana recoiled.

"Begging your pardon, ladies," said the first hand, shooting a warning look at the other man. "I'm sure we'll hear good news any time now. You'll see." He kept his tone positive, but Gwenwhyfar detected the same nervousness in his demeanor.

That same worry permeated the whole town, and it was all she could do not to allow herself to get caught up in it. She hoped this city wouldn't turn into a panicked mob as well. By the looks of things, anarchy waited only for a catalyst.

Over at the dock, Etxarte haggled with one of the *barca* captains. "That's an outrageous price!" he yelled, gesticulating wildly. "I'm only buying passage on *one* ship. Count it: one. Not an entire confounded fleet of them!"

After several more rounds of arguing, he gave the man his sac of money. He returned to their spot with a tired stride. "That man should be charged for piracy."

"You've done well, my guardian," said Gwenwhyfar. "I began to worry if we'd find passage at all."

"The ship departs in the morning," he said. "But we don't have any money left for lodging."

"Let us sell the horse and chariot," she suggested. "They don't belong to us, but I don't see that we have any other choice."

Etxarte nodded, then led the horse and chariot away, disappearing into the hustle and bustle of the forum.

Gwenwhyfar's stomach rumbled. The energy from those meager bits of cheese and olives that morning had long since ebbed. Food vendors were doing a booming business that day, the most they'd done that year. The smells wafted up to her nose, and her mouth salivated with hunger.

A while later, Etxarte returned with a grin. "Good news, ladies. We can eat now."

Æliana inquired about where they would stay that night.

He shrugged. "I'm still working on that."

"I hope we won't have to sleep with animals again," she murmured.

"We will make do, mother," Gaia reminded her. "Once we get to Sicily, we won't have to endure any more hardships."

Gwenwhyfar hoped Gaia was right. She realized that they had not actually *seen* the Villa Duilius. What if the Harappans had indeed moved further inland in Sicily and ravaged the countryside? She kept her worries to herself, however.

They managed to find a restaurant with available seating, and ate their first decent meal in days. With great effort, the ladies tried to eat with the dignity that befitted their stations.

Etxarte maintained no such qualms, and stuffed his mouth full of food as though there were no tomorrow.

For all any of them knew, tomorrow might not dawn.

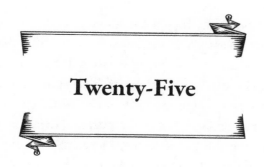

Twenty-Five

MARCUS STOOD ON THE deck of the *Varina*, unmoving as a stone wall. He reminded himself of the words he spoke to the crew: *They're mortal men. They bleed and die like the rest of us.*

What was it his friend Ptah would say? *The Harappans' power is nothing but advanced science. Look, you've even managed to keep them too busy to make any more waterspouts!* He smiled at the memory of Ptah's laugh, which surely would have followed those words.

For each ship the Harappans sank, Marcus made a point to sink one of theirs in retribution. His crew had rammed three enemy ships already. Each time, they backed the trireme away right before the Harappans could board.

They had kept up the fight for hours, loading yet more fiery arrows into the basilisks, cranking them back until they reached the proper tension, and timing their release with the ship's rocking.

He barely maintained that ship for ship count, though. The crew began to tire —aside from old Brutus, no one else had survived a battle of this duration. Every conflict Marcus had experienced thus far seemed like a training exercise compared to this.

But he refused to give ground to the enemy. To his satisfaction, neither did Barca. He had to admit, the Punic commander fought with more bravery and honor than he believed possible for his people. The other captains followed their example. Witnessing the courage of his own countrymen made him proud to be a Roman.

This was Rome they fought for, after all, and she could never fall. They would drive away the Harappans, just as they had done with every other invader, from the oppressive Etruscans to the greedy Carthaginians. Oddly enough, some of those same Carthaginians from the Sicilian War now fought beside them against their common enemy.

"Keep it up, men," shouted the centurion. "Don't get sloppy! Fire!"

The remaining handful of archers loosed their arrows.

Next time we ram them, we must board, Marcus decided. *My men can't last much longer.*

As it was, his and Barca's ships arrived right on time for any hope of influencing the battle's outcome. Most of Rome's initial defenders had sunk to the watery depths.

The crew fought well, every man proving himself. If they survived, he intended to give the rowers their freedom, just as he'd done with those who fought with him at Ker-Ys.

An enemy ship floated into range. It was now or never. "Ramming speed," he ordered. "Ready the *corvus*! Unchain the rowers."

Brutus knew what that last order meant. They were making a last stand. He nodded in approval—better to fight now, before the men succumbed to complete exhaustion.

The *Varina* picked up speed and charged toward her glorious destiny. Marcus stroked the wooden railing at his side. *You have served both Rome and me well*, he told her. *Worthy you are of your namesake, and I thank you. I must ask you to perform one last duty.*

The distance closed. He braced for the jarring impact. Another few seconds...

Three seconds...two...one...

Crash!

Wood splinters shot in all directions, hitting both Harappan and Roman alike.

Marcus balanced himself, drawing his sword. "*Corvus*! Now!"

The grappled plank lowered and latched onto the Harappan vessel. "Board them!"

He rushed forward across the bridge, his marines behind him.

They cut down the opposition along the way. The freed rowers leaped over the side onto the enemy vessel, swelling the Roman ranks.

Fortunately for them, the Harappan commander did not made such a magnanimous gesture toward his own rowers. The prisoners languished below deck, helpless to save themselves. Marcus would try to enlist their aid as well.

In the meantime, he allowed his training to take over. Thrust—block—thrust.

"Cut them down!" he urged his soldiers. "Push them back!"

On his right, and on his left, his men fell to the poisoned blades of their enemy.

A collective cry of pain sounded from the bow. At the first chance Marcus got to look, he saw that a bucket of oil had spilled and caught on fire. The entire bow roared with flames. Men caught on fire, jumping overboard in a frenzy.

Only a matter of time before that fire consumes the entire galley! But he could do nothing at present to stop it.

Someone managed to free the rowers. They rushed from below all around him, wreaking their vengeance against their captors. Marcus almost pitied the Harappans.

Thrust—block—thrust—thrust!

He stayed his sword in mid-swing, realizing he had no more opponents. The ship was theirs.

"Sir! We've won!" Brutus cried.

"I can see that. Put out that fire—"

He grasped Marcus by the shoulder. "No, tribune. The battle! We've won the battle!"

Marcus scanned the seas around him in awe. Sure enough, Harappan galleys sank all around them. Barca's single remaining

Carthaginian vessel, though also in the process of sinking, made for the beach to run aground and save the hands.

Pride swelled his breast. Still surprised, he raised his sword. "Victory!"

A roar of approval met his shout. "Duilius! Duilius!" his men cheered.

Their cry was interrupted by a sudden, heavy rocking, which sent most of them reeling across the deck.

"That wasn't a wave, sir," Brutus noted.

"We're sinking! Back to the *Varina*!"

But when they returned, they found water rising from the lower decks. The *Varina* would soon follow her adversary down to the depths.

Brutus frowned at the collecting water. "They must have fired one of their metal shots before we rammed them. It's no good, tribune." He shook his head. "We can't get to shore fast enough to run her aground."

Marcus nodded stoically. Truly, they had achieved more than he had hoped for. They saved Rome. That would have to be enough.

He climbed to the upper deck to address the crew. "You have done well, men!" he announced. "If ever a victory proved worthy of a triumphal procession, this was it! Rome will always remember us with honor and pride on account of this victory."

"Duilius! Duilius!"

I don't deserve their praise, he thought. *I couldn't save them.* But he did not correct them, lest he dampen their spirits further. "Die well, my crew!"

To make the mood even more somber, rain began to fall from the angry, black clouds gathering above—for once, not the work of the Harappans' spells. Taller and taller waves lapped against their crippled ship. He hoped at least some of his sailors would survive by swimming to the shore.

He watched the boiling sea swallow the bow of the *Varina*. Not for the first time, he felt relieved he had sent off his lady Varina, as he had known all along this was how things would end. She was safe, together with his mother and sister. In that knowledge, he could satisfy himself.

The entirety of the Roman and Carthaginian fleets had perished. But the battle was won. Gloriously won. That should be all that mattered.

I love you, Gwenwhyfar. I only wish I could have married you.

The dark, churning waters engulfed him. Instinctively, he held his breath.

Everything went black.

"COME ON!" ETXARTE URGED. "Or the ship will sail to Sicily without us! And then who will be there to welcome that boy home?"

News of the Harappans' defeat reached Capua not long before the bodies washed ashore near the port town. A feeling of dark foreboding came over Gwenwhyfar. At once, she made for the seaside.

She suspected Etxarte felt the same premonition, and feared that she might discover something he did not wish her to find on the beach. "Where are you going?"

"Please," she entreated. "Marcus might have washed ashore. I'll never forgive myself if I don't make certain."

He tried to harden his expression, but could not hold his resolve against her quivering lips. "Bah!" He threw his hands in the air and let her go. Gaia and Æliana followed her.

The waves pushed hundreds of men ashore, most of them dead before they reached land. Other women and scavengers searched the bodies for their loved ones, or for valuables.

Gwenwhyfar pondered on the all of the lives that had been destroyed, and not just those of the sailors. In homes all across both the cities of Rome and Carthage, families would never see their sons, brothers, and fathers again. Such was the heavy price of war. In that moment, she came to the sad conclusion that in war, there were no winners after all.

"Marcus!" Æliana wailed. "My boy! Oh, they killed my poor boy!"

To Gwenwhyfar's horror, there lay her valiant hero, the waves lapping at his limp form. An intense pang of sorrow struck her right in the heart. How would she live without him?

"No!" The word escaped her lips as little more than a hoarse whisper.

Æliana succumbed to hysterics, and it was all Gaia could do to hold her mother up amid her own sobs.

With trembling apprehension, Gwenwhyfar put her finger to his throat. She thought she felt a pulse, but feared to believe it, lest it turn out to be the rumbling from the sea—or her wishful hopes. No, it came from his veins.

"He's alive!" she cried. "His heartbeat is weak, but I can feel it. Fresh water!" she demanded.

Searching his body for blade wounds, she exhaled with relief when she found none. No poison in his blood.

"Oh, thank the gods!" Gaia exclaimed, her tears turning joyful.

Etxarte crossed his arms and wryly observed, "He has the lives of a cat, that one."

By some miracle, Etxarte managed to secure passage for Marcus on the ship bound for Sicily.

"He's been injured," he told the captain. "You won't have to worry about him eating much or getting in the way."

All the same, the price of an additional passenger cost them a night's lodging. But upon learning of their plight, the first mate was moved with compassion for them, and permitted them to board early to spend the night on the ship.

✕

DIM LIGHT FROM THE town filtered into the cramped cabin as Gwenwhyfar watched her tribune sleep. The others stayed up top as much as possible, avoiding the dank air below. But Gwenwhyfar sat by Marcus' side the majority of the time, giving him small amounts of water from a spoon. She determined to stay with him until he got back to his feet, no matter how long that took.

"I love you, Marcus," she whispered often in his ear. "We'll reach your home soon, where your stewards will proudly present your fine olives for me to taste."

The sea air would do him worlds of good—better than the land air. He might even recover before they reached Sicily. It made her blood run cold to think she had come so close to losing him forever. But even with the tiny window left open during good weather, the lower decks of any ship were always stuffy.

"You should go up top and take some sunshine and fresher air," said Gaia one morning.

Gwenwhyfar shook her head. "No, I want to be here when he awakens."

"You must take care of yourself if you're to be of good to him, princess." She giggled, "Forgive me, but you look awful. Do you want him to see you with those dark circles under your eyes, and your skin pallid from a lack of sunshine?"

"Well..."

"I'll stay with him and send for you if he wakes up," she promised. "Now go on up! You can sit with him again tonight."

Still not enamored with the idea, Gwenwhyfar reluctantly acquiesced. She made her way up the ladder to the main deck. Though this merchant vessel had much more room than a Roman warship, she missed the *Varina*, the elegant trireme Marcus named for her Roman alias, before he knew her real name.

Given that he had washed up on shore, she had most certainly sunk during the battle. Marcus must have gone down with her, believing he would share her watery, dark grave. Thank the gods that hadn't been his fate!

She found Lady Æliana also standing on the main deck, staring out to sea.

Gwenwhyfar stopped in her tracks. The Roman matron considered her a barbarian. It hurt Gwenwhyfar to know that Marcus' mother disapproved of her. Her husband, Gaius, had refrained from giving his opinion of Gwenwhyfar when she met him in Atlantis. But then again, the admiral had not been aware of his son's attachment to her at the time.

"Princess," she acknowledged with a civil nod.

Gwenwhyfar braced herself for a speech akin to Etxarte's lectures about her and Marcus' lack of compatibility, suitability, and whatever else she would surely add on top of it.

"I regret some of the things I said to you the other day," Æliana began.

She blinked. "*Domina*?"

"The enemy soldiers frightened me. The world I knew was ending all around us."

"Never have I met a people so fierce as the Harappans," Gwenwhyfar offered, sympathizing. "My experience was similar when they attacked my home."

"I am grateful to you for saving me and my daughter." The silent *but* at the end was as good as audible.

"You're welcome."

An awkward silence ensued.

"I'll be frank," said the matron. "You and Marcus can never marry."

The words hit Gwenwhyfar like a pillar of marble.

Æliana's harsh expression softened. "You are both young and full of ambition. His admiration of you is well founded. He has always aimed for the loftiest of goals. It's just like him to set his sights on a foreign ruler. I was a young woman once, too," she continued. "Marcus is both strong and handsome, as well as courageous. It's only natural for him to catch your eye."

At first, it was the other way around. But Gwenwhyfar allowed the elder woman to finish.

"You must give him up," she insisted. "Marcus' life is already decided. He must marry a Roman girl. I can see you are a great woman, and I can't help but admire you. But you are also a barbarian. Nothing can change who and what the two of you are."

Gwenwhyfar met her eyes. "I believe a man makes his own fate, my lady." Before Æliana could come back, she persisted. "You praise and insult me all at once. I must be a great woman indeed to have made such a strong impression on you."

"I speak as I find," she said, denying neither statement.

The two women glared at each other. Before either backed down, the cook announced the evening meal.

After the cold silence of their dinner, Gwenwhyfar returned to Marcus' side with a heavy heart. It would sadden him to know his mother refused to give her blessing. That her own family disapproved was bad enough.

"Oh, Marcus," she whispered, kneeling as his side. "You know how much I love you. What are we going to do?"

The darkness concealed her silent tears. She laid her cheek upon their clasped hands and soon fell asleep.

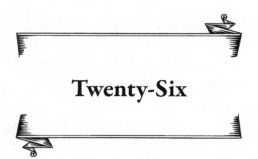

Twenty-Six

WATER.

Oceans of dark, cold, crushing water engulfed him.

In his delirium between planes of existence, Marcus dreamed of Gwenwhyfar, of the rolling hills of olive groves in Sicily, of Gaia and his mother, of his first sea voyage as a boy with his father.

"I love you, Marcus," said Gwenwhyfar's specter. "Return to me, my brave hero."

The warm touch of her lips to his forehead startled him, so far from life had he faded. It was a sweet vision, and he felt grateful to have had it before the time came to face the terrors of the netherworld.

All warmth faded, and the light slowly dimmed into twilight. The last thing he saw was Charon beckoning for a coin to pay for his passage across the Styx.

A sharp sensation of rain on his face ripped him out of his dreams.

He tried to open his eyes, but the water's sting kept them closed. Turning his aching neck, the water rolled down the side of his face. Rain still hit the side of his head, but at least he could now open his eyes. With a few blinks, the sights around him blurred into focus.

He was on a ship at sea—that was apparent to him right off the bat. Only not his ship. He had never before entered this strange cabin. How did get here?

Then he remembered the battle. The sea had swallowed the *Varina*, and him along with her. He managed to rise to the surface, despite the battle draining all of his energy. He survived. Someone pulled him from the water. *Brutus?*

He scoured his throbbing mind to glean more details.

Nothing. He could not remember what happened after sinking from exhaustion beneath the waves.

"Oh, I'm sorry," said a feminine voice—Gwenwhyfar!

The water stopped trickling onto his cheek.

"I left the window open for fresh air. I didn't know the rain would blow in." A dry cloth sopped up the cold moisture pooled around his head. "Better?" she asked sweetly.

His first attempt to speak turned into a coughing fit. "Sorry I'm late, my lady. I was busy getting blown out of the water."

"But you defeated them." Her soft laughter was the dearest sound he had heard in what seemed like a lifetime ago. "You've blown me out of the water with your heroics." She flashed a smile that sent his heart racing.

Warmth continued to fill his body, and his head began to clear. "That was the general idea. I've been trying to impress you since the day we met, you know."

"You mean saving Rome wasn't important?" she teased.

"An added benefit. Something to make my victory all the sweeter."

Her smile faded. "Alright, now that you've impressed me, please don't do that again. Nursing you back to health is an enjoyable diversion, but not worth the price of my earlier worrying whether you'd live or die."

He chuckled, causing him to cough again. "But you're such a lovely nurse. Last time, I was your nurse. I like it better this way."

She pursed her lips together. "I'll bet you do."

As the events of the fight played in his mind, he remembered his loyal centurion. "Brutus?"

Gwenwhyfar encouraged him to lay back down. "I don't know. But I can tell you that most of your crew did not survive. I'm sorry, my love."

He exhaled. That was, of course, to be expected. Between the Harappan's poisoned blades and the rough sees, it would take a miracle for any of the crew to survive. He would learn nothing until he returned to Rome later—several weeks, at least.

He said a silent prayer for his friend, then drifted back to sleep.

THEY ARRIVED AT THE Villa Duilius in Sicily one fine afternoon. Marcus got back to his feet the following day.

He stood in the garden at the pond's edge practicing his strokes with the *gladius*. He exercised his limbs with care, lest he take away strength from healing his body.

His mother had deduced his attachment to Gwenwhyfar, and no doubt guessed what he planned to do. Though she did not approve, she said nothing. That decision lied in the hands of the *paterfamilias*—and they both knew already who held the greater influence over him.

Marcus was not worried about that. He'd proven himself his own man many times over. Even if Gaius did not agree with his decision, he would respect it on the grounds that his son had earned the right to make it in the first place. His dreams of glory were finally starting to come true, yet he could not find satisfaction in his achievements without Gwenwhyfar as his wife.

His mother would not make it easy. But after all he and Gwenwhyfar had endured together, it would prove a trifle matter. Æliana would warm up to Gwenwhyfar eventually—everyone did. The thought made him smile.

"Penny for your thoughts?"

His pulse quickened. He lowered his sword as Gwenwhyfar approached. "I was thinking of you, and your great beauty."

"I'm happy to hear it," she said, a lovely pink hue flushing her face. "I have news for you, but it can wait until you're finished with your exercise."

"I've done enough for today." He gestured for her to sit at a nearby table in chairs on the patio.

She moves with perfect grace and poise, he thought admiring her elegant form from behind while she walked. He could maintain his stance in raging gales and keep perfect balance in combat. Next to her, he felt like an oaf.

He exhaled when he realized he'd stopped breathing.

She sat down, and her smile turned serious. "The Harappans razed Carthage to the ground. Another armada attacked them while Barca stood with you to protect Rome."

Marcus had not even thought about the general. "Did Barca survive the battle?"

"Yes," she answered, her tone grave. "He managed to run his ship aground and save most of his crew."

He pondered the shocking news in silence. Carthage destroyed—and Barca had not been there to defend her! Instead, he'd lost his entire fleet defending Rome.

"His lack of warmth towards us has no doubt turned to ice now," he mused.

"I'm traveling back to Atlantis to learn of any other news before I return to Ker-Ys," she announced. "With any luck, my first letter reached my brothers, and they'll assume I never left," she added with an endearing twinkle in her eye.

Marcus pouted. "You're leaving me again?"

"You sent me away last time. Remember? But," she added another breathtaking smile, "I hoped you'd come with me."

He was instantly smitten. "How can I refuse the regent of Ker-Ys?"

Rome, of course, would need him to help clean up the aftermath. But that herculean task would take several months. Whether they liked the idea or not, the senate could argue by themselves while he finished his recovery in Atlantis.

By the time I return to Rome, they'll finally be ready to do something.

BREEZES OFF THE OCEAN blew through the war council chamber, cooling those who gathered there. Outside, the tropical heat beat down in hazy waves upon Atlantis. Hardly a soul stirred in the city's streets.

It seemed to Gwenwhyfar that it was always hot on the island continent, and she appreciated that the Atlanteans possessed the technology to at least keep their buildings more comfortable. She stole a glimpse at Marcus, noting the dampened neckline of his tunic.

No one could disagree the situation grew more dire by the day.

"There can no longer be any doubt," said Admiral Itza. "The Harappans will come for Atlantis next. See how they've decimated the forces of those around us: Rome, Ker-Ys, and we've just learned they burned Carthage to the ground."

General Barca straightened at the mention of his home. "Carthage still has forces remaining in Hispania," he reminded the admiral. "We're not finished yet."

Gwenwhyfar imagined that had the general not recently won a glorious victory defending Rome, he might have fallen on his sword. But he returned to Atlantis to convene with the allies. He brought with him his young son, Hannibal.

Itza acknowledged Barca's brave words. "Of course. But they keep coming, general. Little else bars their path to Atlantis. Once finished here, they'll move farther westward on to the Mayan lands of my birth."

"I have succeeded in recruiting the Euskaldunak," reported Gwenwhyfar. For an instant, she reflected on the price she paid to accomplish her aim. "I agree with Barca. We aren't finished."

Werta shifted from one foot to the other. "You're right. We're not finished. It grieves me to have to reveal it like this." He looked on at the faces around him. "Atlantis has a new fleet of airships to meet this increasing threat."

Barca trembled with anger. "And you didn't tell us? Duilius and I might have saved our fleets! We might have saved Carthage!"

"I only just found out about them myself," the mayor answered, shooting a look at the Mayan admiral. Itza shrugged. "They aren't fully operational. They'll be ready to launch in a week's time."

"We may not have a week!" Barca turned to Marcus, who'd stood by in silence, listening with his arms folded. "What is Rome's position on this matter, Tribune Duilius? You've not said a word this entire conference."

"I am obliged to point out," said the tribune, "that I'm not authorized to represent Rome at this meeting. I have not received instructions from my superiors or the Senate." He paused. "But if you want my personal opinion as a soldier, I say we're caught between the sea and Hades. In such cases, I always choose the sea, for there I have some control over my fate. While these weapons of war were not authorized, Atlantis has them nonetheless. I say you should use them."

Gwenwhyfar threaded her fingers together. "I must agree with Duilius," she ventured, "on all points." What more could she say? The deceitful deed had already been done. They may as well make use of this resource.

In truth, she felt relieved that a new fleet sailed the seas to fight their enemy's growing power. Before learning of it, their prospects for survival appeared bleak. Now, a new hope emerged that she never believed possible.

Itza turned to Werta. "You see? Even they agree with me. The danger is only beginning. We must take the necessary measures to protect ourselves."

"Very well," Werta resigned. "Since you all concur with the admiral, I'll concede to standing corrected. For now."

Itza's expression softened. "I want you to know, I take no pleasure in your admitting your error, my friend. I've always respected and valued your opinions. I loathe the times we don't see eye to eye. But it is good to hear you now understand what must be done."

"Oh, I understand well enough," said Werta. "I just wish there was another way."

Gwenwhyfar noticed that Ptah, who'd returned to active military service, listened intently to all that was said. He, like Werta, seemed to disagree with Itza's building up their military forces in secret. From his silence, she gathered he'd already argued with his superior over the matter—and lost.

"Sometimes our paths are unfortunately chosen for us," said Itza, more kindly. "When this is over, we can build a better world, where the people are wiser. Our vulnerability is the direct result of our people's own decadence and laziness. Perhaps this is what is necessary to teach them."

"True enough," conceded the mayor. "Though that's the same excuse used by every dictator and law breaker in history. What makes this case different?"

Itza leaned forward across the table. "You want the world to be perfect, Nedril— and that's a noble goal. But the world isn't perfect. It's people like me who give the world the chance to try another day for virtue."

KENDA STOOD IN THE light of the rising moon on a balcony overlooking one of Atlantis' waterways, studying the sky. Thanks to an extended stay in the Mayan lands, he knew every constellation and every star within it. He knew how to find his way from anywhere, to anywhere.

And yet, he felt utterly lost.

Below, a ferry boat drifted by on the canal, ushering a group to their evening activities. The women's laughter echoed across the water. They had not a care in the world, no worries about their future.

To him, the future seemed as dark as the night around him. Enemies from both within and without threatened to close in on his beloved city-state. What had made Atlantis great was her great people. That age of greatness clearly had ended.

He understood that Itza believed he'd done the right thing, the "necessary" thing, as he called it. If they did win the war, what would happen then? The precedent had been set. What new evils would be justified as the result of this example? He astonished himself with his own thoughts—these were the same reasons for the Breizhians and Euskaldunak leaving Atlantis generations ago.

His thoughts were interrupted when he overheard Barca's voice on the balcony above him. The general was speaking to his son.

Kenda retreated into the doorway, not intending to eavesdrop on a family conversation. As he started to close the door, however, he caught words that unsettled him. He left the door open a crack.

"Remember these Romans, Hannibal. For the time being, we must ally with them. But the day will come when we will have our vengeance upon them, as we will the demons of Harappa. Never forget that."

The boy's voice was grave. "I'll remember. What of the Atlanteans?"

"For the time being, we have no quarrel against them. They are people of action, yet they have not made war upon us."

Kenda closed his eyes. He sympathized with Barca; he had lost his own home and family. It took him years to discover that vengeance never filled an empty heart. The situation was indeed hopeless if the allies could not put aside their differences. How much bloodshed did Barca require before he could see that?

In all honesty, he had to admit he once thought along those same lines until as late as his sojourn to India. His prejudice against Shahin had blinded him, to the verge of their deaths. But he found the wherewithal in time to see the bigger picture.

"Something had better change soon," he whispered to the night. "Because the way things stand now, we're all headed for hell."

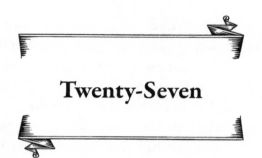

Twenty-Seven

ATLANTIS SHIMMERED in the light of a full moon in a clear sky. Fresh breezes from the ocean had long cooled the streets from the day's heat, so typical of equatorial regions. Street lamps lit the city roads and walkways, though the moon shone bright enough that the lights were not needed on that night.

Gwenwhyfar and Marcus strolled hand in hand. Their time together was precious to them, and they savored each and every moment while they had the opportunity.

Palm fronds above them swayed in the breeze, their rustling mingled with the calls of crickets. They had walked for quite a while when at last they came to the whispering arch. Marcus stopped to admire it.

"This place is dear to my heart, for it was here that you first trusted me. And I have not betrayed your confidence." His voice was warm and deep, like that spellbound night.

"So it is," she agreed. "When did you first trust me?"

Marcus gently stroked her cheek. "From the moment we first met."

She blinked. "Surely you're not so foolish! How can you trust someone you don't know?"

"I saw you for the woman you are: honorable, loyal, and you weren't afraid to stand up for what's right. I never told you this, but on that day, I went to the temple and prayed for you to one day be mine. For all I wished, I never believed it would truly happen."

It was evident in his voice that a twinge of jealousy lingered in his heart over her first having married Petronius.

She brushed a lock of his dark hair out of his face. It had grown since he had rescued her on the high seas, months ago.

"I'll get it cut soon," he said with a boyish grin.

She raised a brow in mock disapproval, and moved her fingers down to the emerging stubble on his chin. "For shame, tribune. What would your superiors say? They'd scold you for spending too much time among us barbarians."

"Oh, yes," he took her into his arms. "And they've been the best times of my life."

"Mine as well." She resisted the urge to melt into his embrace, to tell him over and over again how much she adored every strand on his head. His occasional scruffy appearance of a sailor endeared him all the more to her.

He held his forehead to hers. "You once said that when I asked you to marry me, you'd say yes."

She sighed. "And you said you wouldn't ask me until the war is over."

"I did, didn't I? At the time I meant it. But consider: already we nearly lost each other twice. Who's to know it won't happen the next time we part?" He felt vulnerable, and Gwenwhyfar understood him well enough to know that he never showed this side of himself to anyone else.

"We don't," she admitted.

"The war isn't getting any better. We may not get another chance." He lowered himself to one knee. "There is no other woman for me in the world. Marry me, my beautiful Gwenwhyfar. If you don't become my wife, I'll never have a wife."

If only she could say yes! She longed more than anything else in the world to marry him, the only man she ever truly loved. She loved

Marcus, and he loved her. If she didn't marry him, she knew she'd regret it the rest of her life.

"You don't know how much I wish things could have been different," he rendered. "I wanted to court you in the way you deserve, as a queen, and according to the customs of your people. I'm fully aware of how much that means to you."

He was exactly right. Asking her to give up the traditions of her home, especially those involving courtship and marriage, was expecting a good deal. Yet in all fairness, she already experienced that with Petronius. To repeat it might stir up memories she preferred to remain buried. On the other hand, that had not been exactly the wedding of her dreams, either.

"I wanted to do that for you," he continued with a helpless shrug. "These are the cards life has dealt us. Would you—could you—dare to play them with me?"

An idea came to her—a wonderful idea! She clapped her hands together. "Why don't we strike a bargain? I'll give up Ker-Ys, if you'll give up Rome."

Hope filled his face. "How do you mean?"

"We'll marry now, here in Atlantis as you propose. After the war, we'll reside at Ker-Ys." She could tell he did not like the compromise. "It's kind of like a treaty, wouldn't you say?"

After a moment, he nodded. "That is fair." Then he pouted. "But surely, you won't deny me my triumphal procession?"

"I wouldn't dream of depriving you of that honor," she laughed. "I'll even ride at your side, if you'll let me." She looked up at him from underneath her long lashes.

"You don't know how long I've dreamed to hear say that."

He pulled her close, sealing the deal with a kiss.

MARCUS NEVER IMAGINED getting married in Atlantis of all places.

Marrying Gwenwhyfar? He thought of that countless times—every day since their first meeting, when he believed her out of his reach forever. Now, here he stood, at last living the happiest day of his life.

Ptah walked at his side. "Am I supposed to remind you that you're only a mortal?"

Marcus certainly felt like one of the gods, processing through the streets while crowds of people cheered him on and threw down flowers and confetti from the balconies. It felt like the triumphal procession he always dreamed about, since it bore only a small resemblance to Roman nuptial customs. He'd been tempted to wear his parade armor, but somehow it didn't feel appropriate for his wedding day. Instead, he chose a tunic of fine linen.

Far behind him, Gwenwhyfar held her guardian's arm, looking every part the goddess in her flowing pale blue gown, her soft hair falling in dark curls down her shoulders.

And soon, he thought, *she will be all mine.*

Ahead stood the whispering arch, where Gwenwhyfar first learned to trust him, where he first dared to hope he might win her heart. He turned to see if she was thinking of that same memory. The beautiful smile she flashed back told him she did remember.

The setting sun bathed his bride and everything else in a glamorous, golden light, dancing off her tiara and jewelry. Marcus reminded himself to breathe.

"Relax," said Ptah. He turned to walk forward.

"I have you to thank, my friend. Without your encouragement, I might never have worked up the courage to pursue her."

Ptah laughed. "As I said then, name one of your sons after me."

"Consider it done."

He slapped the younger man on the shoulder, a huge grin on his face. "Who knows? It might happen tonight, eh?"

Marcus felt certain his own face flushed a deep red. It did not stop him from laughing along with his friend.

IT SEEMED THAT ALL of Atlantis turned out to watch what the heralds had dubbed the wedding of the century. Fanfare trumpeted the approach of the procession. Every dignitary and official showed up—they wouldn't risk disappointing the people, or the disapproval of their peers.

Admiral Itza agreed to put aside talk of war for a day; and General Barca delayed his return to sea to attend. "Not for Duilius," he made it clear, "but to witness the happiness of Lady Gwenwhyfar, though I can't understand why she wants a Roman when she can have any other man she chooses. Who understands a woman's mind?"

On the crowded streets, people complained of the difficulty in seeing over the heads of others. "They should have hired a float," one man remarked. "They spared none of the other expenses," said a woman.

His shop closed for the event, Shahin looked on with no small amount of amusement as Jak the reporter pushed his way around the masses, jotting down each and every detail.

Jak moved closer to the tailor and offered his greetings. "You know, of course, her dowry is in question?" he inquired, throwing out his line.

"I did hear something along those lines," Shahin acknowledged. Jak's fishing for information amused him, even if he didn't intend to give him anything to catch.

When the younger man tired of waiting for more, he continued. "Duilius' family may not acknowledge the marriage, either—dowry or not." He waggled his eyebrows.

"Is that so? I'm intrigued to read more in the evening news."

Jak understood he would get nothing out of the Persian. Either that, or he decided to move on to easier game. Making his excuses, he disappeared into the crowd.

After the ceremony, Shahin intended to head back over to his shop and prepare for the rush of dress orders that were sure to pour in by the next day. He already knew what his customers would say. "I want a dress like Princess Gwenwhyfar's, but not one that looks like it's copied." As with every fashion craze, they would expect him to work his magic.

He then noticed a young woman crying near his side. "I just love happy endings. Don't you, Mr. Shahin?"

Miss Irune, he remembered. A girl who nurtured a crush on him from the day she first entered his shop. Currently, she was one his biggest customers.

She should set her sights on one more worthy, he often thought since he discovered her infatuation.

"You will have your own happy ending one day, my dear," he assured her. With a bow, he left the scene before things had the chance to morph into something that might hurt her feelings—and his business as a result.

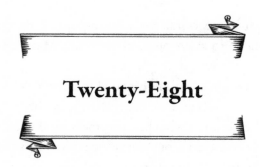

Twenty-Eight

THE WEDDING PARTY REACHED the steps of the house Gwenwhyfar and Marcus would share for the remainder of their stay. Tropical flowers and streamers of blue, green, and silver decked the doorway, extending along the architectural features.

She watched Marcus ascend the steps, where Mayor Werta waited. His military upbringing taught him to school his features even during life's most violent storms. He held himself up taller to give the appearance of confidence, but she could tell his heart swelled as much as hers did. Longing and adoration for her shined in his handsome brown eyes.

How different this all felt from when she wedded Petronius. She was a trembling girl of sixteen when her brothers gave her to a virtual stranger from a foreign land. Though a kind and honorable man, Gwenwhyfar didn't love the Roman senator. At the time, she feared her life neared its end. Oh, she'd had no idea how close her prediction came to what would unfold in the days that followed!

Yet despite the trials she endured up to this moment, here she stood, about to marry the man she truly loved.

Nothing had succeeded in stopping them from being together, not war, not social and familial expectations, not their hailing from different peoples.

Seeing his love for her as he waited in front of the door, somewhat impatient, caused everything around them to blur. The sea of eyes fixed upon her disappeared. A tear spilled down her cheek. Then another.

Etxarte's gentle touch on her arm grounded her. "I'd ask you if you're certain you want this, but I already know that question is futile." He held her for the last time before she would belong to Marcus. "You mean as much to me as a child of my own flesh."

When she pulled back, she saw his eyes shining with unshed tears. "Are you alright, guardian?" she asked.

"It's this blasted tropical sunlight," he grumbled, wincing as he spoke. He pinched the bridge of his nose and sniffed. "It's not as bright back home, you know. Anyway, I'm just happy my girl's happy."

She gave him one last squeeze, then climbed the steps to take her place next to the man soon to be her husband.

Mayor Werta looked up from his scroll. "Are you ready?" Performing marriages seldom fell under the mayor's jurisdiction in Atlantis. But upon learning their plans, Werta insisted on claiming the privilege. A verbal consent between the bride and groom fulfilled the legal expectations of the island continent.

To satisfy Roman and Breizhian traditions, Marcus and Gwenwhyfar clasped their right hands, while Etxarte fasted their hands together with a silk rope.

The elder man gave the Roman a look of warning. Gwenwhyfar guessed they'd already exchanged heated words earlier, and the glare served as his final warning.

Werta placed his hand over their joined hands and announced his approval of the union. He turned his attention to the spectators. "I invite the people of Atlantis to feast and dance in honor of our distinguished couple tomorrow at midday."

Since the couple would have only a few days together before they must return to their perspective homelands, the mayor agreed to oblige them to but a few hours of public appearance the next day after the ceremony. The crowd cheered.

He held up his hand for silence. "Well?" he asked Marcus. "Isn't it a Roman custom to kiss your bride?"

"Hurry up, boy!" Etxarte called. "Before I change my mind."

"What are you waiting for?" urged Ptah.

Her husband turned to her with a devilish look. Her skin tingled as he pulled her into his arms, his warm lips gently meeting hers. She barely heard the roar of approval from those who gathered, so loud did her blood pound in her ears.

Once she caught her breath, she uttered the traditional words of a Roman bride. "Ubi tu Marcus, ego Marca." *Where you are Marcus, I am Marca.*

"I appreciate that," he whispered.

Sweeping her up into his strong arms, he carried her across the threshold.

He closed the door behind them, and the world outside slipped away. "Do you remember when you told me your name?" he asked over his shoulder, still facing the door.

"It was here in Atlantis. How could I forget?"

"I was so nervous." He chuckled. "I thought you might refuse to tell me."

"You would have learned it that night in any case," she reminded him, her heart skipping a beat when he turned toward her.

"It wouldn't have been the same. I wanted it hear it from you." He wore that same smirk, both triumphant and smitten, as he had at the party on that night in the Hanging Gardens.

Gwenwhyfar thought it the most adorable expression in the world. "That's why I decided to have mercy on you, tribune."

"Will you have mercy on me now?" He fell to his knees and wrapped his arms around her legs, burying his face in the folds of her gown. "A free citizen of Rome knees before no one, but I kneel before you, Gwenwhyfar."

"Oh, Marcus..." she trailed off, realizing that he was past teasing. "Why do you doubt my love for you?"

"Because you can have any other man you wish."

She blinked, uncertain of his claim's veracity. "I've married you," she giggled. "What further proof do you need?"

He rose to his feet. "What further proof indeed?" he asked, cradling her face in his hands.

They both knew they had only a few days together afforded to them before they must return to their respective lands, to carry on the fight for the world's freedom. Neither had an inkling of what the future held for them. But she would not think about that now. Now, there stood only Marcus, her husband, the love of her life.

He drew her trembling lips to his—the beginning, at long last, of true love's first blissful union.

AFTER THE WEDDING FEAST, Werta went to his office. Now that he'd enjoyed the joyous distraction, it was time to figure out what to do about his dilemma.

How was he going to tell the people that their government had deceived them, used their taxes without their permission to build weapons and warships about which they knew nothing? Many politicians might be tempted to pass off the blame and spin the situation into a coup to mow down his opponents.

But Werta was an honest man. He took the job because he cared about serving his city-state.

What he really wanted was to go to the back room of his wife's tavern and drown his worries with drink and Ezria's soothing words of encouragement. Although, he did not need to go that far; a bottle of honey wine waited in the cupboard next to his desk.

No, he had a speech to write. Filling a cup of water instead, he walked over to the window and rested his head on the glass. "I'm in over my head," he whispered, his breath clouding the view for a moment. He closed his eyes. "What a fool I was, to think I alone could make a difference!"

"You can still make a difference, mayor," said a strange, feminine voice. "You are not alone."

Werta opened his eyes to see the reflection of his visitor behind him. Not believing the first take, he turned. His cup shattered to pieces at his feet.

A beautiful, strange-looking female stood before him. She held a trident, and wore the traditional woven kelp dress of the ancient Atlanteans. As he stared at her pale skin with patches of scales, her flowing aquamarine hair, her eyes the color of the sea, Werta knew what sort of creature she must be.

And yet, he could hardly believe it. *Mermages* were a myth! Nonetheless, there she stood in his office, having risen out of the small fishpond in the corner.

She looked like a young girl, but that told him nothing. Mages of the sea were said to live a thousand years.

"I am Viviane."

Her silvery voice met his ears like the splashing of a brook. Hardly surprising, since legend also said they possessed the uncanny ability to pass through water from one location to another. This one appeared to have done just that. The tiny fins on her arms shrunk as the water dripped off her skin, until they disappeared altogether, rendering her nigh human.

"We seldom choose to have contact with your kind."

Werta nodded rapidly in agreement, still unable to form words.

"But the situation of the world is dire," she continued. "As a Follower of Erykanis, it is my duty to inform the Mayor of Atlantis that certain forces are working toward the destruction of the Island Continent."

He found his voice. "Don't I know about that," he snorted, remembering Itza's going behind his back to build weapons of mass destruction, on top of the ever growing Harappan threat.

"Don't you?" she asked, her sad, enchanting eyes searching his face. "My order, as you may already know, predicted these events via mathematical calculations four hundred years ago."

A sense of foreboding welled in his stomach. "You aren't the only ones," he conceded.

The door flew open, after only a brief knock of warning, and Kenda Ptah strode in. His mouth fell open when he beheld Werta's visitor, his initial purpose forgotten. "Sons of the pharaohs!"

Werta cleared his throat. "Um, Ambassador Ptah, this is Viviane, a Follower of Erykanis."

Ptah studied the *mermage*. It seemed to Werta that a magical and mysterious moment passed between them. Understanding, perhaps? Did this girl also possess the ability to read minds? For once, the opinionated captain found no comment to utter.

Viviane broke the silence. "I bear a message from my order. The threat to Atlantis lies both from outside enemies and from within. Forces have been set into motion that cannot be undone."

"Are you saying there's nothing we can do?" Werta did not want to believe her prediction of impending doom.

"To prevent Atlantis' end, no." He saw that she looked upon him with sincere sympathy, like a mother having to tell her child no when she likewise believed the circumstances unfair. "But you can ensure that end counts for something."

"Can't you be more specific?" he persisted. "I don't understand."

"You will," she maintained, "when the time comes. This I may tell you: you no longer stand alone. We will do all we can to aid you."

With that, she stepped into the water, her fins and scales re-emerging. Lifting her arms, she wove the liquid around her form and vanished. The suspended drops fell onto the surface like a gentle rain, and after a few seconds, the waterfall resumed its previous flow.

"Gone!" Ptah exclaimed, hovering at the edge of the pond. "What an exquisite woman!"

Werta blinked. *How can he think of female beauty in the face of such grim tidings? He, of all people!* Before his thoughts turned into words, however, an idea came to him. "Do you think so?" P

tah came back to reality. "Well..." he trailed off.

He lifted a brow, prompting the Nubian to continue.

"...I have no objection to meeting her again," he finished quickly, his ebony skin taking on a ruddy tone.

A smile spread across the mayor's face. High time to even the odds—or his name wasn't Nedril Werta!

He folded his fingers together. "Ambassador, I have new assignment for you."

IKAL ITZA, ADMIRAL of Atlantis' proud Navy, stood in the darkness among ancient ruins outside the ringed city. Others trickled into the group waiting to watch the sun rise. He had observed this tradition in his homeland for as long as he remembered.

The first rays of the summer solstice would undulate down the pyramid's steps, manifesting the shadow of the serpent god. Known as *Kukulcan* in his native Mayan tongue, Itza recognized that the being he worshiped took on various names throughout the world.

Here in on the Island Continent, worship of any gods had virtually died out long ago. Or so, most believed.

These particular ruins survived as a testament of Atlantis' "ignorant past," a monument used to educate school children. Little did most Atlanteans suspect that an active cult made use of the temple and its grounds. Human sacrifices were, naturally, out of the question if the sect wished to avoid scrutiny by the authorities. But an animal here and there would not be missed.

Manik, a young fisherman, and one of the few other full-blooded Mayans who resided in Atlantis, placed a hand on Itza's shoulder.

"Any luck?" the admiral inquired.

Manik shook his head. "We've searched every rock of those mountains—twice."

Though he expected that answer, Itza felt frustrated anyway.

A part of him began to doubt if the portal to the Otherworld mentioned in the *Chronicle of the Sentinel* existed. According to the source, this gateway lied somewhere in the Atlas Mountains, and would enable the faithful to establish direct contact with Kukulcan. It was clear that the Kali deity favored the Harappans, and Itza determined to find his own all-powerful ally.

Manik and his supporters had scoured the mountains. Thus far, the gateway eluded them.

"The only place we haven't searched is Mount Vukad."

Vukad, the ancient name for Vulcan's Forge, the last remaining active volcano in Atlantis.

"How can it be there?" Itza muttered, not expecting a response.

"There are no springs on that mountain," Manik said, reading Itza's thoughts. "If there were, they would burn up. Gateways must have water."

I know that! Itza bit back the words on the tip of his tongue. "Kukulcan will show us the solution," he returned instead, rubbing his eyes. "Keep searching. I'll consult the *Chronicle* again. Perhaps I missed something?"

All conversations halted. Dawn approached.

As Itza watched the Feathered Serpent's shadow dance down the steps of the pyramid, his faith renewed. Kukulcan would show him the way. He simply needed to stay the course.

The Harappans would rue the day they chose to serve Kail.

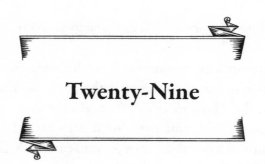

Twenty-Nine

THREE MONTHS LATER...

"I can't believe you delayed your triumph over a woman," Brutus remarked, adding, "If it's not out of line for me to say so, sir."

The scuttlebutt among the few surviving sailors—both Roman and Carthaginian—claimed the tough old salt swam to shore after the battle while fighting off sharks and drowning Harappans.

Marcus laughed. "I'm delaying in order to re-establish relations with Rome's newest ally," he corrected. "I want the Breizhians to join in the celebration. Besides, she's part of my victory. I want to see the adoration in her eyes as she sees me honored."

The two men walked to the water's edge, surveying the final building stages of their new ship, a *quinquereme* Marcus named *Gwenwhyfar*.

Brows had lifted at his choice.

No officer named a warship after his wife— especially not a barbarian wife. Varina was a common enough name, and easily explained. But this... That Tribune Duilius put on hold his own triumphal procession through the streets of Rome in order for her to witness the celebration added to everyone's astonishment.

"How is your bride?" the centurion inquired.

"She's well," said Marcus, his grin widening. "We exchange letters often. I can't wait to go back and see her again."

The smallest smile tugged at the corners of Brutus' mouth. "You'll grow out of it."

"There is where you're wrong, my friend." He scanned a report, nodded in approval, then handed it back to the carpenter.

"I look forward to seeing the Fortress of the Deep again as well," the older man confessed. "To drink that cider again. Best I've ever tasted." He smacked his lips in anticipation.

"You should try their mead, too," Marcus suggested.

Brutus took a breath to answer, but his attention diverted to the edge of the shipyard.

Marcus turned to see a messenger boy gingerly descending the stairs to the dock. He headed right for them. "Perhaps that's from your lovely wife now?"

Sure enough, the messenger placed his scroll into the tribune's waiting hands. He thanked the boy and, as the sender expected no response, sent him on his way.

It was not from Gwenwhyfar.

But that did not surprise him. Since returning from Atlantis, practically everyone in Rome sent him well wishes and salutations. That, in addition to his correspondence with his superiors. He should not have gotten his hopes up.

Marcus squinted at the wax seal. "Scipio?" That *did* surprise him.

"What does the old windbag want?" Brutus growled.

He broke the seal with a shrug. Marcus' father had served as censor with Scipio, but beyond that, he had no official connection to the man. His lesser known connection had been with Scipio's floozy daughter—but as far as he knew, Scipio did not know who hired the assassin to remove her along with Secundus.

Or did he?

The note was short and to the point, like the killing strike of an assassin's dagger, driven right into the back.

"Bad news?"

He barely heard Brutus' question above the whirling confusion of his mind.

His body went numb, and he felt the scroll slip from his fingers. If Scipio sought revenge for his daughter's death, his coup succeeded.

"Tribune? What's wrong?"

Marcus felt as though he had strayed into a nightmare. *Time to wake up*—but no, the centurion's hand on his arm told him this was all too real.

He managed to choke out a response. "Ker-Ys has fallen to the enemy."

Coming Soon...

ATLANTIS
On the
Seas of Fate

LUCIUS CORNELIUS SCIPIO stepped off the deck of his ship onto a snow-covered dock. Rome's current treaty with Ker-Ys ensured that her sovereigns could not refuse him aid, despite their leaders' personal opinions toward him.

He took a risk, sailing this far north in winter for supplies. But thanks to an Atlantean storm detection device on loan to the Republic, he successfully navigated the stormy waters of the North Atlantic (and he hoped to rely on Roman ingenuity to duplicate and improve the technology). Surely, this city of Atlantean exiles lay far enough out of the Harappans' range this time of year to be as safe a place as any.

Scipio's breath froze in the frigid air as he exhaled. Soft, lacy flakes fell around him, landing in his hair and in the folds of his uniform.

Among the descending particles, Gwenwhyfar Meur, Regent of Ker-Ys, stood waiting to meet him.

She is so young, the Roman veteran observed. Or maybe he was just getting old.

Though she looked weary, her chestnut eyes had not lost any of their previous fire. Recalling their last encounter in Atlantis, he thought she looked more like a regent now in her fine cloak, her diadem visible from underneath her hood.

"Consul," she greeted.

He bowed in return. "Princess Gwenwhyfar."

"Please walk with me along the shore, while we make the arrangements for your repairs."

It was not a request, and he understood by the flicker of fear in her eyes that she had more to tell him. His curiosity piqued, he complied with her request, offering her his arm out of courtesy. A thin layer of snow crushed atop the rose granite sand as they left the wooden planks.

"What a shame that you've come in winter, as it does not show our city to its best advantage," she said in a tone of false pleasantry.

The moment they were out of sight of the docks, her casual expression faded. "We have only a few moments. We are under enemy occupation, Consul. You must leave now before you are captured."

Scipio lifted a brow. "We did not see any ships." He would never think her a liar, but he found it difficult to believe the Harappans would refrain from their usual custom of pillaging every city they captured.

"Their ships are hidden in the north bay," she explained. "There isn't any more time. Go, before it's too late."

This was astonishing, but he could see in her face that she spoke the truth. "What will happen to you, my lady?" he asked. Though she was the wife of his daughter's murderer, he no longer placed the blame for that on her.

She held her chin high. "I expect they plan to execute me at some point. But they will not get the chance. We're revolting tonight." Her mouth turned up into a grim smile. "They will rue the day they set their sights on Ker-Ys."

"I believe it," he returned. "You are a courageous woman, and you have earned my respect and admiration. I wish you success." Bowing, he hastened back toward the docks.

If only he could help her somehow! But they both knew Rome could not afford to lose any more leaders or ships.

As he had predicted a year earlier, the Harappans would indeed save him the trouble of exacting his vengeance on Marcus Duilius. Scipio despised the man, and the haughty tribune would finally pay for wronging his family. Yet the triumph rang hollow.

His admiration for Lady Gwenwhyfar had stayed his hand from carrying out his vengeance. Upon meeting this remarkable young woman, he found he could not bring himself to cause her pain merely because the man she loved was his political enemy. My, he was growing sentimental as well as old.

"Wait, Scipio."

He stopped, and turned to face her.

She hesitated. "I wonder if you would be good enough to do me a favor."

"Name it," he said, for he did not wish to see her humble herself.

"Would you please deliver a message to my husband?"

She must know that she asked a great deal. He also realized it took a great deal of humility for her to ask him—of all people—for help.

Bitterly did he understand that he no longer required retribution. For Duilius, his adversary conveying his fair lady's last words to him would prove torture enough.

"For you, I would consider it a privilege," he answered.

She smiled, grateful tears shining in her eyes. "Tell him," she said, struggling to keep her voice even, "that I faced my death with courage. Tell him he is the only man I have ever truly loved."

Committing her words to memory, he nodded.

"Swear it," she demanded, her voice faltering.

"As a Consul of the Roman Republic, I swear to deliver your message exactly, my lady." He added gently, "Accept my assurances once more that I will not retaliate toward Duilius or his family."

"Thank you," she whispered.

A deep male voice echoed from down the path toward the city, causing them both to start. "Princess! Come here at once!"

Her eyes widened. "It's him." The alarm in her voice twisted the Roman's insides. "Go before he sees you! I'll distract him while you sail away."

Scipio thought it loathsome and cowardly to leave her there at the disposal of some Harappan swine. But he knew better than to ask her to come with him. She would never abandon her people.

If he didn't escape, other allies might fall into this trap. Every warship was needed if they were to have any chance of winning this war.

As the oarsmen pulled his ship back toward the stormy Atlantic, he watched her hurry up the path toward her captor.

They had escaped. Even if they were discovered now, it was too late for the enemy to pursue them. He made a fist and pounded the railing, uttering the most vile curse that came to his mind.

That lady of Gaul possessed more Roman spirit than most of the Roman women he knew. Plebeian or no, if Duilius was indeed a true Roman, his pride in such a wife would outweigh his grief at her loss.

Don't miss out!

Visit the website below and you can sign up to receive emails whenever Jennifer McKeithen publishes a new book. There's no charge and no obligation.

https://books2read.com/r/B-A-HGEF-WGAAB

BOOKS 2 READ

Connecting independent readers to independent writers.

Did you love *Atlantis On the Tides of Destiny*? Then you should read *Shahin: Escape from Persia* by Jennifer McKeithen!

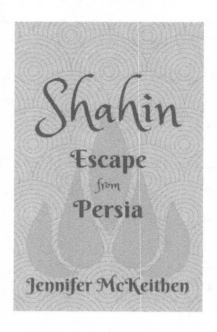

A prince on the run ...A girl with a terrible secret ...A sorceress hungry for power ...An unforgettable journey.Sixteen-year-old Shahin's father is dead. Now he must flee the wrath of his wicked aunt and leave behind everything he knows. But he can't do it alone.His guide is Amrita, a beautiful girl who hides a terrible secret. With her help, they elude the palace guards and navigate the treacherous mountain pass out of Persia. As they near Amrita's homeland, Shahin develops strange, thrilling feelings for her. But can he risk trusting her with his heart as well as his life?The past youth of Atlantis' most enigmatic resident revealed at last! Following the traditions of classic young adult fantasy and pulp fiction, Jennifer McKeithen weaves a new tale of danger, first love, and betrayal in this coming of age adventure.

Read more at www.jennifermckeithen.com.

Also by Jennifer McKeithen

The Antediluvian Chronicles
Atlantis On the Shores of Forever
Atlantis On the Tides of Destiny

Standalone
Shahin: Escape from Persia

Watch for more at www.jennifermckeithen.com.

About the Author

Jennifer grew up in beautiful south Louisiana. Her earliest memories were in New Orleans. Living in "America's first melting pot" taught her to appreciate culture, cuisine, and music from a young age. Her lifelong fascination with Ancient mythology and Medieval folklore remains another influence on her writing. She and her dashing husband, Japheth, live in Kansas City, Missouri.

Read more at www.jennifermckeithen.com.

CPSIA information can be obtained
at www.ICGtesting.com
Printed in the USA
BVHW071108230719
554154BV00001B/71/P

9 781393 609780